Marine Artist

Melrose Lane Series
Book 3

MK Dwyer

A Marine is a Marine. I set that policy two weeks ago - there's no such thing as a former Marine. You're a Marine, just in a different uniform, and you're in a different phase of your life. But you'll always be a Marine because you went to Parris Island, San Diego or the hills of Quantico. There's no such thing as a former Marine.

—GENERAL JAMES F. AMOS, 35TH CMC

Contents

Melrose Lane Series

Marine Artist is the third full-length book in the Melrose Lane series. While Marine Artist can probably be read as a stand-alone, follow the link below to start with Book One.

Book One: Marine Firefighter on Amazon

Book Two: Marine Brother: A Christmas Novel

Book 2.5: Marine Luck: A St. Patrick's Day short story

Book Three: Marine Artist *(you are here)*

Book Four: Marine Protector *(coming soon!)*

Chapter One

Jesus

"**W**anna come back to my place for pizza and sex?"

"Excuse me?"

"Do you have something against pizza? We could do burgers. I'm not picky."

The woman sitting on the barstool next to Jesus looked stunned for a moment before she threw her head back and laughed. He was just about to ask if he could buy her next drink when someone cleared their throat behind him in an obvious attempt to get his attention. He turned to see a younger, leaner man about his height standing there with a raised eyebrow and a what-the-fuck expression on his face.

"My bad, man. Didn't realize she was unavailable."

The man took his time looking Jesus up and down, and while they sized each other up, he wondered if he was about to get kicked out of the bar for fighting. It wouldn't be the first time that he ran into a hot-headed kid with a daddy-shaped chip on his shoulder and something to prove. Ten years ago, he would have been just as eager to show off his moves, but not anymore. Not only did he have no desire to fight over the girl, but as he got older, he realized it was a poor and disrespectful use of his training.

While enlisted, he'd poured hours and hours of discipline into advancing to black belt in the Marine Corps Martial Arts Program. When he became a civilian again, he'd kept up his training for exercise, and over the years, the practiced motions had become a form of meditation. A way to shut out the static that always threatened to invade his mind like an old television with inadequate bunny ears.

Then the man smiled, and Jesus realized he'd jumped to the wrong conclusion.

"No harm done. Would you like to have a drink with us? I don't mind sharing." He winked.

"Oh." Jesus looked back and forth between the pair, still wondering how he went from the failed pickup line to a threesome invitation. "*Gracias*, but I'm looking for a little one-on-one tonight."

"That's cool. If you change your mind later, the offer's open—if we're still here."

Jesus paused as he smiled at the man and glanced back at the woman. "Sure thing."

He walked away and found War alone at the bar. "No luck?"

Jesus chuckled. "More like too much luck." He

had nothing against threesomes for other people, but they weren't for him. That was actually the drawback of going out with War. Women often wanted to go home with both of them. They were close, but not quite *that* close.

"What about you?"

War grunted and flashed Jesus a smirk. "Don't worry. I'll find someone." He held up a highball glass of amber liquid. "Wanted a minute first, just me and Johnnie."

War only drank Johnnie Walker Blue Label to celebrate or commiserate, and it didn't take a genius to figure out which one he was feeling tonight.

"What's up, man? Anything you want to talk about?"

War huffed a short laugh. "Nah. Just in my head too much tonight. I'll empty my glass, and then my balls, and be right as rain by tomorrow."

Jesus just shook his head at his friend. "No doubt, War. No doubt."

It was a winter evening in San Diego, which meant nothing in terms of weather. A little cooler, but still not cold. A little darker, but still not dark. Definitely not cold or dark enough to deter anyone from a hook-up bar on a Saturday night.

He ordered a Johnnie for himself and sipped in silence with his buddy until both their glasses were empty. Clapping his hand on War's shoulder as he stood up from his stool, he made a mental note to check on his friend later. The bar wasn't the place to ask what was going on, and neither one of them would appreciate going home unsatisfied because they spent too much time attached at the hip, pouring their hearts out to each other and giving themselves whiskey dick.

"Catch ya back at home later?"

War smirked. "Yeah. Don't wait up."

"Same, asshole. Same."

Jesus took a lap around the bar, weaving his way through the tables before choosing a girl sitting alone at a table with multiple drinks in front of her. By the looks of things, she was either attempting to get very drunk, or she was holding the fort for her friends. She was pretty, with straight brown hair just past her shoulders. He wasn't close enough to see her eye color yet. Not that it mattered.

She seemed average in looks and build. Not the type to stand out in a crowd, but not exactly a wallflower either. These were the girls he usually went for. The quiet types that he had to coax out of their shell with a little banter. The ones who took compliments with grace and maybe blushed a little. The cute girls who enjoyed his attention as much as he enjoyed theirs.

He glided onto the seat next to her before she could protest. "Hey, sweetheart. What kind of bagel are you?"

"Oh, that seat's ta... Wait. What?"

"What kind of bagel are you?"

"Uh. Did you say 'bagel'?"

"You see. I figure I'm an everything bagel," he leaned in close enough to whisper in her ear, "because I satisfy everyone."

Bless her. She giggled. That line wasn't even in his top five.

He extended his right hand. "Jesus."

She shook his hand with a funny look on her face. "Jesus? As in 'born in a manger'? Jesus?"

He threw his head back and laughed as he held on to her hand. "Yes. Women everywhere call out my name during sex, no matter who they're with." He winked, and she giggled again. "And you are?"

"Megan."

"Hello, Megan. Are you here alone tonight?" He knew she wasn't.

"No. My friends went to the restroom. They'll be back soon." He wasn't sure if she added that last bit for his benefit or her own.

"And they left you here all by yourself?"

"Yeah. I just moved in with them, but they were already really close. I'm usually just the third wheel when we go out."

"Well, we can't have that. How about a dance?"

"Oh, I don't know. I promised I'd watch their drinks."

"Looks like you're finished with yours though. How long have they been gone?"

"A while. Maybe there's a line."

"Of course, there's a line. There's always a line. If I know that, then they knew that too when they ordered before leaving you to sit here and watch the ice melt."

"Well, yeah, but I can't just leave the drinks either. What if someone messes with them? And they'd definitely lose the table."

"Another table will open up, and what if I can solve the drink-problem?"

He got the attention of a passing waitress and handed her the roommates' drinks. "Would you tell Ryan that two girls are going to come to the bar and ask to have these drinks remade? He can put the drinks on my tab, but only these two drinks. It's under Jesus, and the girls' names are…"

He looked at Megan, expecting her to fill in the blank, but she just looked at him strangely when he paused.

"Megan, what are your roommates' names?"

"Oh. Macey and Daisy."

He held his tongue and didn't ask if her roommates were Pitbull puppies, but only just barely.

"Got it."

He thanked the waitress and slipped her a tip as she left to relay his request to the bartender. He stood and extended his hand to Megan in a silent gesture to join him.

She took his hand and allowed him to lead her to the dance floor. The song playing was upbeat and somewhere between hip-hop and pop. Jesus wasn't really sure. If it wasn't country or rock, he was lost, but he appreciated any song that made a woman's hips move and shake. They found their rhythm quickly and kept dancing through each new song. Half an hour of bumping and grinding later, his dick was aching behind his zipper and begging for release, and her hooded gaze told him she was equally affected.

He pulled her closer so she could hear him over the loud music. "What do you say we head back to your place?"

She pulled away a little and looked him directly in the eye, like she was gauging his trustworthiness. "I don't even know your last name."

"It's Benavidez. What's yours?"

"Harris. What else will you tell me about yourself, Jesus Benavidez?"

She enunciated every syllable of his name like a taunt, and it made him smile.

"Hmm. Well, I'm a tattoo artist, but I love to create art on canvas as well. If you're wondering about the accent, I'm originally from Texas. My mother's name is Esmerelda, but everyone calls her Esme, and I have four older sisters. And while I love them, mi papa, and the rest of *mi familia* dearly, I have no plans to move back."

Offering information on his large—mostly female—family was usually all it took to put a girl's mind at ease. Like someone with four sisters couldn't be a *complete* slimeball. Right?

It helped that his sisters really would skin him alive if he ever mistreated someone.

"Four sisters? And you're the youngest and only

boy? That's intense."

He barked a laugh. "Yeah. It certainly was growing up, and it still can be when I'm home or they all decide to call me in one day. I swear, they either have some sort of weird sixth sense or they're coordinating their calls to purposely drive me nuts."

He chuckled good-naturedly about his family. He really did love them, even if he was happy not to live too close. As Megan put it, he was the youngest and only boy. He had to carve out his own life or suffocate.

"And you're a tattoo artist? That's interesting. If your hair wasn't so long, I would have guessed you were military with how fit you are and the way you carry yourself."

He smiled and shrugged. "That must be a side-effect of living in San Diego. You can't go ten feet in this town without running into a Seaman or Marine." There was no need to tell her how close to the mark she was. He rarely went into his military background with a hookup.

"True. You're just very—built."

Her delivery made him bark a laugh again. At this point, his cheeks hurt because he was smiling and laughing so much with this girl. She was fun and frank. "Just dedicated to the gym. Tattooing is a very sedentary profession. I have to combat all those hours sitting hunched over in one position or I'd grow a gut pretty quickly. What about you? What do you do?"

"I'm an executive personal assistant."

"Oh? To anyone that I would've heard of? That kind of personal assistant?"

"Yes." But then she sealed her lips together and grinned.

"Ah, a woman who can keep a secret. I like it."

She laughed. "Is that what you're looking for tonight? A secret rendezvous?"

"Nah. It doesn't need to be a secret, but it will be a one-time deal. I'm not looking to start anything here. Just a little fun."

She opened her mouth to respond just as someone cleared their throat behind him for the second time that night. He had to hand it to the girl, tapping her foot behind him. She managed to be so passive aggressively loud that he heard both noises over the thumping base of the music on the dance floor.

When he turned, he saw a blonde with her arms crossed and mused that she'd be really pretty if she wasn't looking at him like he was a cockroach under her stiletto.

"Where are our drinks, Meg? You promised you'd watch them."

He was about to speak up for her when she beat him to the punch. "You were taking forever, and I wanted to dance. This is Jesus, by the way. If you go to the bar and give the bartender your name, he'll remake your drinks on Jesus's tab. All right? Maybe next time, order your drinks after a trip to the ladies' room, not right before." The blonde opened her mouth to respond, but Megan cut her off. "Now, Jesus and I are going to get out of here. I'll see you two back at the apartment later."

It wasn't until then that he even noticed the other girl standing behind the blonde. She was a darker blonde and decidedly less hostile looking.

It was she who responded to Megan. "Umm... okay. Yeah Megan. We'll see you later."

He wrapped an arm around Megan and veered her off the dance floor, giving a quick nod to War on his way out. The night had turned out just the way he'd wanted, and Megan was a great girl. Too good to be a one-night stand, but he knew that was still all he could promise. Leaving the bar with a pretty girl on his arm, he should've been excited to continue an already fun night, but he just felt tired and weary.

Chapter Two

Jesus

Three Months Later

Sitting back on his stool, Jesus gauged his client's reaction as the man admired the newly inked lion running the length of his muscular torso. If the beaming smile on his face was anything to go by, then they were both pleased with the final product.

He smirked to himself.

Not one to brag, he'd admit it *was* some of his best work. He would never attempt a piece he couldn't accomplish, but he'd been skeptical when this new client said he wanted "a lion made of fire." Three sessions and countless hours later, that vision plus his skill equaled a kick-ass piece of art that they both could be proud of.

The reds, oranges and yellows of the tattoo gave the illusion of movement like a flickering flame had come alive in the form of a fierce lion. Even he'd been impressed as it took shape on the man's skin at the end of his machine.

After clearing and cleaning his station, covering the tattoo, collecting his fee, and ushering his client out the door with aftercare instructions, he turned around to the empty shop and took a deep breath. He was the last one there and the lion-of-fire was his last scheduled tattoo of the day—his very long day.

It was barely nine on a Thursday night in early spring, but he was more than ready to get out of there. The shop manager had quit a week prior at Black Sails Tattoo Studio, and until they hired a new manager, the owner declared they would only stay open for walk-ins on the weekends. He was more than happy to close early and get the hell out of there while he could. Something was off with him. Burn-out, maybe? He knew he needed a change but hadn't figured out what that change was yet.

Sweeping and locking up the tattoo studio only took a few minutes, and he was driving down Broadway in his black 1974 Chevrolet Chevelle before he decided where he was going. It was a crisp, clear evening, much like most nights in San Diego, and the options were limitless—if he was so inclined. He wasn't.

Maybe that was the change he needed to make. When was his last spontaneous moment? His last adventure? Hell, when was the last time he'd even taken the scenic route home? Most nights, he chose to take the same route that passed up the same pub, and he stopped in nearly every time.

After all, there certainly wasn't anything waiting for him at home.

His roommates were busy with their own lives. War, with his unique ability to be as big as a house, had started moonlighting about a year ago as a bodyguard for extra cash. And Adam, with his off-the-charts computer skills, would most likely be holed up in his office tracking someone or something down for a client. They'd all met while serving in the United States Marine Corps but hadn't become good friends until they moved in together after their enlistments. Well, until Adam bought a house and took in tenants to offset the obscene mortgage needed to own a home in Southern California.

He and War were Adam's first tenants, but the fourth bedroom had housed a few different guys in the last couple of years. Some for a few months, and some for a few weeks. The last long-term occupant of that room was a firefighter named Will, whose son, Joe, came to live with them as well. Will had served with a friend of Adam's and they'd all liked him when he came to check out the room.

The circumstances of Joe's arrival weren't what they first seemed, and Jesus felt terrible for making snap judgements about Will's ex-wife, Theresa. He couldn't understand how a mom could dump her son and take off without caring, but it turned out she cared enough to keep both her son and her ex-husband safe. It was admirable, and though he still considered her half-crazy, she was at least an excellent mom to the kid he'd grown to love like his own... if he were to ever have any.

Somehow, everything had turned out all right for them, though. Will fell in love with the perfect girl for him, and they were about to get married. Theresa fell in love with another Marine and had a baby. They even bought houses across the street from each other and just down the street from Jesus and the guys. It was an odd set-up to him, but it seemed to work out for them. Theresa obviously still loved getting under Will's skin whenever she could, but somewhere along the way he went from blowing up at her to laughing it off. Well, most of the time. Whatever magic happened there, Jesus was glad Joe had both his parents back and that he'd picked up some pretty cool bonus parents along the way.

He was happy for them all, but damn, was the house quiet ever since the kid moved out. Was that really almost a year and a half ago? He used to rush home just to play Xbox with War and Joe. Maybe he was getting too old to have that much fun playing video games but having an eight-year-old around had made him feel like a kid again. Not to mention, it distracted him from the fact that he was lonely. He'd never admit that to anyone, even under duress, but that didn't mean it was less true.

Not counting the occasional detour to a woman's bed for a few excellent hours, he worked out; he went to work; he went to the pub, and he went home. He hadn't gone on an actual date in too long. To say he needed a change was probably an understatement.

People assumed just because he was naturally a happy, flirty person with an easy smile that he had a black book of women at his beck and call, but in reality, the opposite was closer to the truth. Sure. He got laid on a regular basis, and that was beyond awesome, but he'd reached the age where it would've been nice to wake up next to someone more than once—or at all since he usually didn't sleepover.

In the Marines, his duties as a mechanic filled his days and art filled his free time. When he left the Marines and started his apprenticeship to become a tattoo artist, art became his day job— or night job most days—and he never picked up another hobby. Even his classic car didn't take up much of his time because he left most of the work to the professionals. He needed something else that kept his hands busy in his off time because regular, nearly anonymous sex didn't count.

He parked his car and walked the familiar path to the front door of Kelly's Irish Pub. He'd lost count how many times he'd crossed the threshold of his usual watering hole. Past the few tables scattered about the moderately sized pub, the leather stools and worn wood of the bar welcomed him like a friendly smile. But it was the beautiful girl behind the bar who always stole his attention.

Stacey Landon welcomed every patron like family. Well, everyone except him. He wasn't sure what he did to deserve the sneer she gave him, without fail, each time he saw her. And no matter how many times he tried to talk to her, the most she gave him was, "What can I get you?" and the like.

He sat down on his favorite stool directly across from her—happy to see it was vacant and the pub wasn't busy—and waited as she washed out a glass. Her eyes were intent on her work, but he knew they were a dark, rich brown. Her matching dark coffee-colored hair was long with full, loose curls. Just once, he wanted to see her hair straight to know just how long it really was. Better yet, if he could get his hands on it, he'd pull a curl down and watch it bounce back up.

And her hair wasn't the only thing he'd love to watch bounce. Her hourglass figure reminded him of the 1950's pin-up girls he used to paint on the side of helicopters. The kind of figure that promised no matter which way he positioned her, he'd get to watch either her tits or her ass bounce as he moved inside of her. Sometimes he wondered if the girl could read minds. Maybe that was why she had a problem with him. Stupid pickup lines to make girls laugh aside. He always made sure to act like a gentleman around women, but his thoughts were rarely—read: never—pure.

"What'll it be?" she asked without looking up.

"The usual, *mariposa*."

She huffed, but grabbed a tulip-shaped glass, placed it at an angle under the tap on the wall, and tipped the Guinness handle towards her. The way she stared at the glass as the russet liquid climbed to the top would've caused Satan to flinch. He knew the look was meant for him, even if he didn't know why.

Setting it upright, she tended to another customer while the beer settled. He couldn't help but watch her as she walked up and down the bar, pouring drinks and conversing with everyone but him. She was a great bartender, friendly, welcoming, and knew her shit. Kelly's was lucky to have her.

She came back to his Guinness, topped it off and brought it over to him.

"Six bucks."

He extended his card towards her, gripped with two fingers. "Keep it open."

She nodded, swiped his card, handed it back, and walked away.

Well then. He sighed and pulled out his phone. It was a habit more than anything. He didn't even know what he was looking for besides distraction.

After a few minutes of scrolling social media and a couple of drinks of his beer, he looked up as a woman sat next to him. She was a pretty, slender blonde, and he was officially dead inside because she did nothing for him. She smiled at him, so he politely smiled back, but he couldn't bring himself to strike up the expected conversation or even one of his silly pickup lines. He didn't normally pick up girls from Kelly's—don't shit where you eat or something like that—but a little flirting never hurt. For once in his life, though, he had nothing to say to an attractive woman.

Clearly, she was as surprised as he was. When he didn't take the bait and respond to the flirtatious looks that she'd flung in his direction, she left in a hurry with the drink that Stacey served her.

He looked up and caught Stacey's eyes. She was also surprised. A glutton for punishment, he winked at her and laughed when she huffed and walked away.

Chapter Three

Stacey

Just when Stacey thought she might be wrong about Jesus Fucking Benavidez, he proved her right all over again. He was a regular at Kelly's, and a regular Casanova too. She'd lost count of how many women he and his buddy, War, had flirted with since she started bartending there almost a year ago. Jan, one of the waitresses, told her he even took home his roommate's girlfriend one time. Something his roommate probably didn't know, considering they were still friends, and the couple was still together.

She was done with men like that. A man like that ruined her life, took everything from her, and then left without looking back. Relationships had been a minefield for her ever since.

A customer trying to get her attention brought her away from the depressing memory lane she'd wandered down. After almost eight years, just the thought of Robby made her want to hurl a stool through a window, and the man who had just winked at her reminded her of Robby much too much. Handsome and funny. The kind of guy who had everything he could ever want and everyone eating out of the palm of his hand, but it was never enough. Charming if he was still interested, but cold and cruel when he wasn't anymore.

Unfortunately, it was a slow night at Kelly's, and he was one of less than ten patrons in the pub that evening and only one of three sitting at the bar. His name was Jesus, not *hey-soos* like one might think, but *gee-zus* like "Christ". At least, that was what his friends called him.

They even called him "Buff Jesus" sometimes, which was a fitting description of his physique, hair, and beard. Not that she was looking. She assumed there was some story there, but she wasn't eager to hear it. The less she knew about or dealt with that man, the better. The man whose beer was almost empty. *Damn it.*

She walked over to him. "Another?"

"*Si, por favor, mariposa.*"

Grumbling at the nickname, she poured another Guinness, placed it in front of him, and added it to his tab. He'd called her "*mariposa*" almost as long as she'd worked there. Google told her it meant "butterfly", but she didn't know why or how he came up with it and had no desire to ask. Well, some, but not enough to voice the question.

Still standing at the cash register in front of him, she felt his eyes on her and looking up, confirmed it.

He smiled when their eyes met, and if she wasn't

already immune to guys like him, she would have swooned. He was the kind of guy who smiled with his whole face—ear to ear and forehead to chin morphed into an utterly disarming look. He had the fullest, kissable lips of any man she'd ever seen, obnoxiously white, straight teeth, and his eyes were deep, dark brown orbs worth getting lost in. *Good thing I know better.*

The backwards LSU cap over his long hair should've made him look like a bum, but instead gave him sexy Jason-Momoa-vibes. She'd wondered more than once why he wore baseball caps from LSU almost exclusively. Did he or a family member go to Louisiana State University? Was he from the state? If so, what brought him to San Diego? She was curious, but again, not enough to ask. Not enough to risk getting swept up into his orbit. It was dangerous there.

A sheet of paper broke their eye contact when the bar manager, Kelsey, shoved a calendar page in her face. "Schedule for next week!"

Stacey skimmed the page and huffed. "What the hell, Kelsey? You gave me like no hours. I have a little thing called rent, and my landlord is funny about wanting it every month."

"Yeah. Sorry. Jan needed some extra hours, and she's been here longer, so…"

"Are you kidding me? She probably just lost too much at the casino, and I don't care how long she's been here. She breaks no less than five glasses a shift and still lives with her mother. I need my regular hours more than she does."

"This week is what it is, but I'll take that into account for next week."

'Take that into account'. What does that even mean? She huffed for the eightieth time that night as she jammed the schedule into her back pocket and bent down behind the bar to grab a new rag. She was in the mood to angry-clean. There was no way the night could get worse, but she just had to stick it out for a few more hours. Then she could forget all her worries as she soaked in her tub. Her apartment wasn't the best or in the greatest part of town, but she rented it for two reasons: the proximity to work in her price range and the glorious soaking tub. The same tub that was calling her name.

She stood up from crouching behind the bar and instantly locked eyes with Jesus. He looked like he had something to say, but she was not in the mood to hear it. She moved to the other end of the bar and pretended to wipe down the bar top. It didn't really need it, but she did.

After only a short reprieve, she noticed him waving her down with his credit card in hand. She rolled her eyes. As much as she wanted to, it wasn't like she could ignore a customer who wanted to pay for their drinks. He could put the card away, though; she didn't need it to close out his tab.

She printed a receipt for him to sign and brought it to him. Never wanting to stand over the patron as they gave her a tip, she started to walk away.

"Wait, Stacey." He paused, then added, "Please."

"What?" At least he'd used her actual name and said the magic word.

"I overheard your manager cut your hours next week."

"Yeah. So?"

He smiled like she was going to be sorry for her attitude, which only made her bristle more. "We're looking for a full-time manager. Ever worked in a tattoo studio before?"

Crap. That would be a dream job if she ever thought she'd be able to have one of those. Dammit, she *was* sorry about throwing around the attitude. "No, but I worked in a hair salon for a while." *Ugh. Why did I say that? Like they're the same at all. And now, he knows I'm not really qualified.*

He smiled again. Damn him. "It is really similar. Making appointments. Knowing how big a block to schedule based on what they want. Inventory management and whatnot. The difference is we encourage all our employees to be tattooed, but I know that's not a problem for you, *mariposa*."

He winked. Damn him twice. That was where the nickname came from. "How did you know about that?"

"Last St. Patrick's Day, you all wore matching crop tops and the little butterfly tattoo on your hip kept peeking out above your shorts. It took everything in me to keep from staring at it all night. I'm surprised you didn't notice."

"I'd only been here a week then, and the place was packed to the gills. I'm surprised I remembered my own name by the end of the night." She laughed, then realized who she was talking to and stopped. "So, this job."

"Right. We open at two tomorrow afternoon. Can you come by then? Fill out an application, meet the owner, see the shop... All that."

"Yeah. No problem. I don't have to be here until five, anyway."

"Perfect." He finished signing the receipt that she'd almost forgotten about. "See you then."

"See you." She paused as he got up from the stool and started to walk away. "And thanks."

He looked into her eyes. "Don't thank me yet, *mariposa*. But you're welcome to thank me anyway you please when you get the job." He winked at her and walked out the door before she could say anything.

What was she getting herself into? She'd spent the last year avoiding him at all costs and barely giving him the time of day only to find herself considering a job working very closely with him. She was an idiot.

Chapter Four

Jesus

Jesus woke up with a smile on his face. He'd almost forgotten what it was like to look forward to something. Just the possibility of seeing Stacey outside of the pub was enough to put a pep in his step as he worked out, got dressed, and ran to the grocery store. They were so low on basic necessities at the house that the toilet paper they were using was a roll he'd swiped from work to get them by until one of them could find the time. Don't even ask about paper towels or cleaning supplies.

Arriving at the studio nearly an hour before it opened, he was the first one there, but he wanted plenty of time to set up for his first client and be the one to show Stacey around the place when she got there. He didn't know why it was so important to him, except that it would force her to finally acknowledge his existence.

While the reason behind her cold shoulder eluded him, that didn't dampen his desire to thaw it. In fact, her stubbornness increased his resolve to break through and find out what she had against him.

Another tattooist and the resident piercer both arrived through the back door while he was setting up, but it was the bell over the front door that brought him to his feet. He smiled when he turned the corner into the lobby and saw Stacey standing there. She was turned away from him, admiring the large canvas paintings on the walls that showcased the skills of the shop's artists.

Most shops had tattoo samples referred to as "flash" on the walls, but their studio felt more like an art gallery up front with cozy offices for appointments in the back. He'd never been so thankful for those paintings. Her distraction gave him a moment to ogle her figure dressed in skintight jeans and a long-sleeved top that skimmed the top of her jeans and barely covered her middle.

Her trim waist and wide hips always brought the most lude thoughts to his mind. Too bad her lower half was usually hidden by a bar top. All the more reason to get her the manager job at the studio. Hips like those deserved to be seen. He wasn't a saint, but he wasn't crass, either. He could keep his thoughts to himself, only voicing them at the right moment when the object of his lust was beneath him, and he was whispering in her ear.

She turned to catch him staring at her ass and huffed. He smiled, she huffed again, and his smile grew. She never hid her contempt for someone, and he liked that about her even when *he* was that someone.

"Miss Landon, thanks for coming in. Jeff Randle, the owner, should be in soon, but I can show you around and explain what the job entails until he gets here."

She looked around the room, then past him before locking eyes with him again. "Is anyone else here?"

He smirked. *Is she afraid to be alone with me? Fucking adorable.* "Beau, our piercer, and Dillon, another tattooist, are setting up their stations for the day. I'll introduce you." He motioned in the direction he'd just come from. "Right this way."

As she walked past him, he caught a whiff of perfume and immediately knew he'd never be able to forget it. He couldn't name it or even identify the scents it contained, but it bewitched him, nonetheless. She looked like sex on a stick and smelled good enough to eat.

She turned around to look at him and only then did he realize she was talking to him while he was lost in his lust. "What?"

"Ugh. Typical." She rolled her eyes. "I asked how many tattoo artists worked here."

"Five, including me and the owner, plus one apprentice and one piercer. The apprentice shares a space with the owner since neither need to use it much, so six stations total. I guess we'll have to figure something out when he's promoted, but don't tell him that." He winked at her, and she rolled her eyes, but he kept going as if he hadn't noticed. "We rotate hours, so there's usually two to six here, depending on the time and day. Like today. It's Friday, so right now there's three, but later there will be at least five to handle the first of the weekend walk-ins."

"Okay. And is it the shop manager that schedules who works when?"

Good question. "We've worked out a regular set schedule between us, and when we know we're going to be out, it's up to us to get someone to cover for us. But there's also an 'on call' schedule that the manager uses to call in replacements when someone calls in sick or just doesn't show up. That's few and far between, though. You're more likely to call someone in because we're slammed with walk-ins. Luckily, we're all pretty keen to come in if there's a guarantee of work waiting for us."

"So, what is the schedule for the shop manager?"

"It's pretty flexible. The shop is open about seventy hours a week and the manager is here for about forty of that. Jeff just asks that you're here for either opening or closing most days to help the artists with the shop set-up or clean-up."

"So, I could schedule my hours here around my hours at Kelly's and keep both jobs? I like working there, but if Kelsey gives me another schedule like she did last night, I'll never make ends meet. And working both jobs might even allow me to get a little ahead."

"Yes. That would absolutely be doable."

"Great! Where do I sign?" She smiled and laughed, and the fact that it was because of something he said just about made his whole day.

"Hold up there. I need you to fill out an official application, and maybe you want to meet the owner and the other guys to see if you like us."

The smile left her face. *Oh right. She doesn't like me.* "Yo, Beau! Dillon! Where are you guys?" It only took a glance to see they weren't at their stations, so he assumed they were in the breakroom.

They walked into the main area where the staff took their breaks and held staff meetings, and when Beau and Dillon saw Stacey, their smiles grew. Beau was lean and stood at about six feet tall. His piercings and tattoos made him look older than his twenty-three years, but Jesus figured that was the point.

Dillon was around the same age, but taller than Beau by a few inches and easily twice as wide, with muscle definition that only came from dedication. They were good friends with similar easy-going personalities, who couldn't have looked more different on the outside.

"Down boys. This is Stacey. She's applying to be the new shop manager, and you know Jeff's rules about canoodling the managers. Beau. I'm looking at you after you ran off the manager before last."

"That wasn't my fault. She got a better job."

"Bullshit. She loved it here but couldn't stand to stay after the two of you called it quits."

Beau muttered something under his breath, but Jesus didn't care enough to ask him to speak up. He'd made his point. He turned back to Stacey, who was visibly perkier after his exchange with Beau. "Stacey, allow me to introduce you to Beau and Dillon. The scrawny one on the right with the holes in his head is Beau, and the big guy on the left is Dillon. Beau is our resident piercer, and Dillon is a tattoo artist who specializes in some of the most realistic black and gray tattoos you'll ever see. But if that wasn't enough, he's also training as a piercer to take some of the pressure off Beau."

She stepped up and shook both of their hands just as the back door opened and Jeff walked in. "Nice to meet you both."

Jesus motioned to Jeff as he walked towards the group. "And this is Jeff, the owner and occasional tattoo artist. Jeff, this is Stacey Landon. She is applying for the shop manager position."

They shook hands. "Hey, Stacey. Have you filled out an application? Do you have any questions?"

"Not yet, and Jesus has answered all my questions so far."

He puffed up a bit at the mention of his name on her lips. "I was just about to have her fill out an application, but I thought she might like a tour first."

"Good idea, Jesus. She should definitely know what she's getting into before she fills out that application." Jeff grinned at Stacey and told her he looked forward to reviewing her application before heading into the office and shutting the door.

"What exactly did he mean by that?" She looked leery after Jeff's comment.

"Nothing. Just that the guys can be crude sometimes, but I've seen you handle the drunks at Kelly's. You'll be just fine here. Trust me."

She smiled at him, and the room lit up. Every little smile she gave him felt like a point in his favor, erasing whatever he'd initially done to make her hate him.

Stacey

Wow. A compliment. Not a flattering word to get into her pants, but a *real* compliment. That was unexpected.

Jesus handed her an application, and she thanked him as he showed her to the table in the breakroom where she could fill it out. When she was done, she dropped it off in Jeff's office, spoke to him for a few minutes about her experience and left without saying goodbye to anyone else, namely Jesus.

She had a decision to make. Not only about whether she wanted the job but also about whether she wanted to work so closely with Jesus. She may have judged him harsher than he deserved, but she wasn't completely wrong about the man. He was a cad. A womanizer. A sweet talker. A flirt. And she knew that he'd left the bar with his buddy's girl. What kind of man did that? What kind of girl, for that matter?

But what did she know about relationships? She'd only ever dated one guy seriously, and that ended so badly that she'd self-destructed. When she first got to San Diego, she partied constantly, made all the wrong friends and slept with whoever. At the time, she'd thought she was damaged goods, and it didn't matter what she did anymore because there was no coming back from what she'd already done.

It was her Aunt Brenda who'd sat her down and told her to snap out of it. That her life was still worth fighting for, but if she didn't turn around on the path that she was heading down, then she really would regret her choices. She didn't change her ways overnight, but that talk was the turning point for her, and she matured a lot in the months that followed. Since then, she'd gone on a few dates and scratched the occasional itch, but she still couldn't bring herself to get close with anyone emotionally. She couldn't get hurt a second time if she never opened her heart again.

No one was asking her for her heart, though, just offering her a job. Even that wasn't on the table yet. She was getting ahead of herself. Like always.

She arrived at the bar almost an hour before her

shift, but sometimes Kelsey would go ahead and let her clock in if they were busy. By the looks of the packed parking lot, she wouldn't have to wait long before Kelsey gave in and asked for her help behind the bar. Jan had the shift before her, and she was slow as molasses and usually itching to leave before happy hour hit.

Hours later, her dogs were barking up a storm, so she retreated to the employee breakroom to sit for a few minutes. Well, "breakroom" was a stretch. It was a supply closet with a couple of chairs in it, a table barely bigger than a postage stamp, and a few lockers where they could stash their purses. Stacey just preferred not to carry one in the first place. Then, she only had to frequent the cramped, musty room when she was escaping the bar area.

When she returned to her place behind the bar, a familiar face was waiting for her.

"Oh good. I thought I'd missed you."

"No such luck."

He cocked an eyebrow at her, and she flinched. She had to remind herself to tone down the snark. Jesus was the reason she might have a new job soon, and she should be grateful for that, no matter who he was.

"Anyways, Jeff took a look at your application, and he wants to offer you the position." He passed her a classy-looking black and white business card. "Call him to set up a time to come by and fill out all the paperwork. You can talk salary with him then too. Pro-tip: Aim high. I don't know what you make here, but Jeff expects the shop manager to live close to the studio, and he'll pay you well enough to live in the city with no problem. Catch my drift?"

All she could do was nod as she accepted the card and the advice. She already lived in the city, but in a crap apartment, and money was still tight. Maybe she could move to a better one. It would still have to have an amazing tub, though. She wasn't giving up her tub for all the tea in China.

"Oh, and try to do it this weekend. We're closed on Mondays, and he wants you to start on Tuesday."

"Tuesday? That's fast."

"If it's too quick, we can wait a bit, but the sooner, the better."

"No. No. It's perfect timing."

"Good." He smiled at her, and she was so excited, she smiled back, surprising them both.

"Now how about that Guinness?"

She was already reaching for a tulip glass before he finished the question.

When she set it down in front of him, he immediately picked it up and took a sip with a smack of his lips and a sigh, like it was a refreshing soda. She giggled in spite of herself, and he grinned like she made his day.

"You're so good at that, *mariposa*. It will actually be a shame to come here one night and you're at the studio instead."

"You act like I'm the only one allowed to pour

you a beer."

"You are. It just tastes better when you do it. It's your sweetness or something. Not that it's ever directed at me, but you know…"

Damn. Awkward. "Sure." She rolled her eyes. "Let me just follow you around to every bar in San Diego and on every date from now until eternity." She laughed at her own sarcasm, glossing over the fact that he called her "sweet".

"Wouldn't be too hard. I only go to one bar these days and I can hardly remember the last time I went on a date. But if I made the date with you, then all my problems would be solved."

"Oh please, I've seen you leave more than once with a girl on your arm." She was choosing to ignore the part where he practically asked her out.

"Like I said, lately that hasn't happened and those aren't dates, anyway."

"Then what are they?"

He shrugged. "Getting laid."

She scoffed. *Why am I not surprised?*

"What? A guy has needs."

"'Needs'? That's such a guy thing to say. A woman has the same needs. We're just a little pickier about how we fulfill them."

He nodded. "Sure. That's true for the majority of women, but I assure you, there are plenty of men and women who don't fall into their respective stereotypes."

"I don't know about 'plenty'. Men are still men."

"Yeah. I guess we are. Some, then. Is 'some'

okay?"

"Okay, 'some'."

By that point, they were both grinning. She wanted to be mad at him for his 'needs', but he made it hard. And admittedly, their conversation had become absurd.

"How did we get here?"

"I have no idea."

"Oh right, I asked you out, and you ignored me."

"And you're cocky enough to bring it up again."

"Not cocky. Confident."

"Well. Sorry to burst your bubble, but I'm not interested."

"No?"

"No."

"Why not?"

Because you're exactly who I could never date. "You mean, besides the conversation we just had?"

He chuckled. "Yeah. Besides that."

"Because we're going to be working together, and I don't date guys I work with. Plus, didn't you mention Jeff had a rule against it, anyway?" It was mostly a bullshit excuse, but the real reason would bring questions she'd never answer.

He was silent for a moment, like he was pondering her explanation. "Okay. That's fair. I'll keep that in mind in case you go running and screaming from the studio in a week."

"What? Why would I do that?"

"No reason. It's a lot to take on, but I'm sure you can handle it."

"Damn right I can." *I think.*

"I like the can-do attitude. Keep it up and you'll succeed at the studio for sure."

"Thanks." She smiled at him. The compliments were nice, but she wasn't dumb enough to let them go to her head.

Walking down the bar, she attended to a few more customers to get away from his attention. Of course, she returned to refill his beer, but never stuck around to let him strike up another conversation.

The ruse was that she was too busy. The real reason was she still had no desire to get too close to the man.

When he finally closed out his tab and left, she felt like she could relax and finish her shift. She just felt super-charged around him and on-guard. In the past, it made her feel more in control to keep him at arm's length and never give him the opportunity to charm her, as he was so good at doing. They would be working together though, and she'd have to come up with a better strategy to guard her heart and emotions from the Casanova.

Chapter Five

Jesus

He glided into the house with the same lightness and excitement he'd woken up with. Despite ending on a weird, silent note, his day had been filled with all things "Stacey" and she'd actually held a conversation with him. Hell might not be frozen over yet, but the temperature was definitely dropping.

Hearing him come in, Adam stepped out of the kitchen.

"What are you humming?"

Was I humming? He hadn't even realized. "Don't mind me. I'm just going to shower and head to bed."

"Hey, hold up. We need to talk 'new roommate'. The last one moved out a month ago, and we haven't rented the room out yet. As much as I've enjoyed the quiet, it'd be nice to split the mortgage four ways again instead of three."

For one reason or another, they'd had a string of temporary roommates since Will moved out. The people who'd occupied that room in the last year had all either only needed a short-term place or hadn't been the right fit to stick around.

"So, rent it out. It's your house. War and I just rent here."

"Oh, come on. You don't just rent here. You've both lived here almost as long as I have, and you're my friends. I want your opinions. I don't want to pick someone that you and War are going to end up hating."

"Well, line up some interviews. I'll give you my schedule this week and War can give you his, so you know when we're all free. Let's get some fresh meat in here."

Adam laughed. "All right, 'fresh meat' coming right up. Can you do Sunday? I have a guy eager to see the room, but I can't get a straight answer out of War."

"I can do Sunday morning. I have an appointment with a client lined up for the afternoon. Speaking of War, when was the last time you saw that fucker?"

"Not sure. I only catch him in passing since he started his latest assignment."

"Same. I guess that means it's going well."

"Yeah, I guess, but do you think we'd hear about it if it wasn't?"

They both said, "No," at the same time and laughed. War was not one to open up or offer up *feelings*. Though Jesus suspected he felt more than most people, the hulk of a man just didn't speak his mind often. One thing was for sure though, when he did speak more than a grunt, people listened. He had a voice you could place in a crowd of a hundred people. It was low and smooth and made everything he said sound like he was spouting sonnets. Jesus had personally seen him charm women just by saying mundane shit in that voice of his.

Jesus, on the other hand, talked to everyone. He could probably talk to a wall and stay entertained. That skill came in useful as a tattoo artist. Not everyone in his chair wanted to talk, but it helped some people pass the time and keep their mind off the needle scratching at their skin.

"Well, I gotta get to bed. Want to join me at the gym in the morning?" Jesus asked.

"You mean meet you in the garage and workout together?"

"Yeah."

"Then why not just say that?"

"I don't know, but you knew what I meant."

"Just barely. Whatever. It's too late to argue the point with you *and* get up to workout with you."

"So, that's a 'yes'?"

"I guess it is. You definitely make the workout go faster and feel less like work." Adam chuckled.

Jesus smiled. He'd take that as a compliment. "Is six good for you?"

"Six? As in A.M.? Really? On a Saturday? You? I assumed working out with you meant I'd be late sitting down to work, but yeah, six is perfect."

"Well, I've got errands to run before work, and

I'd like to get there early."

"Early? You?"

"Yes. Quit acting surprised about everything."

"Sorry. It's just… surprising." He smirked. "Who are you and what have you done with Jesus-my-own-time-Benavidez?"

"I have my reasons."

"So, that's how it's going to be?"

"That's how it's going to be."

"Oh yeah? What's her name?"

"Her. Who?"

"The girl who makes you want to be better?"

That shut him up for a moment. He *did* want to be better. How did one person have such an effect on another? Was it even her, or the prospect of detouring from the path he was on to a better one? But nope, either way, he was not ready to spill the beans to Adam.

"No one. I mean, there's no one. I've just got a client coming in tomorrow that I want to be ready for." It was a half-truth, so it would sound like the whole truth. He did have a client coming in, but he was already completely ready for the appointment.

His sole reason for wanting to go in was to be there when Stacey came in to speak to Jeff. Damn, he had it bad for someone who barely tolerated his existence, but he really didn't care.

Of course, it was his luck that she showed up while he was in a lengthy session with a regular, and he never even saw her. Instead, Jeff caught him at the end of his shift to inform him she would be starting on Tuesday. It wasn't like he expected her to suddenly jump his bones and fawn all over him, but he thought they were at least moving towards the friend zone where she would stick her head in his station to acknowledge the person who told her about the job in the first place.

He wanted to kick himself for overanalyzing everything like a hormonal teenager, but everything about her threw him for a loop and he rarely knew which way was up with her. It left him excited and dumbfounded at the same time.

"One other thing," Jeff looked around the empty breakroom, but still motioned for Jesus to follow him into his office before continuing, "I've decided to take a step back from the studio."

Surprised, Jesus was too stunned to speak before Jeff went on.

"I'll still keep the occasional appointment like I do already, but I won't be in as much. In fact, I'd like to leave most of the day-to-day operations to you. Though this place doesn't need a whole lot of handholding."

Still unable to make his brain catch up with the words coming out of Jeff's mouth, Jesus stammered, "Uh, why?"

"Why you? Or why leave?"

"Both."

Jeff laughed. "Okay. I want to open another business. It might be another tattoo studio. It might be something else, but I can't stay in one place for the rest of my life. Running this place has been fun and I love being my own boss, but I want to grow and expand my horizons. And I want you to take over here because you've been with me from the beginning, and I couldn't have done it without you. Frankly, I'd love to take you to my next place too, but your passion is artistry, and you'd just hate me if my next place is a restaurant or something."

"Well, I've seen some amazing art from chefs too, but not the kind of art you want to make every day. You have a heart for this place that I just don't share anymore. It should be run by someone who cares, and there will be a bump in pay, obviously too, but we can discuss that later. I just wanted you to know what was coming."

"Wow. I don't know what to say. I mean, I get it. You've always been a little restless. I'm surprised you've stuck it out here as long as you have." Jesus was teasing and Jeff knew it. Jeff swatted at him as Jesus chuckled. "I'm flattered you want me to take it over, really, but can I think about it a bit?"

Jeff clearly wasn't expecting him to say that. "Uh, sure. Yeah. Whatever you need."

On his way home that evening, he got a phone call from Will, who asked if Joe could spend the night with his uncles.

Jesus smiled. He loved that kid. He didn't care if they weren't really related. He would claim that kid until his dying day. He told Will he was almost home and would talk to Adam and War when he got there if they were home.

He should've known it'd be a moot point, though. Walking in the door, he found Joe already there, asking Adam himself. Living right down the street had its perks.

Adam looked from Joe to Jesus and smirked. "War won't be home until tomorrow, but I say it's okay if you do."

"Yeah. Sounds like a blast to me!" He'd said that last part to Joe, who whooped and hollered and ran out the front door without closing it behind him.

Jesus chuckled as he shut the door and joined Adam in the living room. "I guess he's going home to pack."

"I assume so."

After living with them for a few months, Joe was still pretty attached to his "uncles", but it was good for Jesus too—therapeutic even—to have the kid over. Joe saw the world so simply, and spending time with him was just uncomplicated. Occasionally, it was nice to escape reality and play video games like a teenager again.

Sometime around midnight, after hours on the Xbox, Jesus was so tired he could barely see straight. Maybe it was nice to escape reality like a teenager, but he was definitely not a teenager anymore.

He paused the game and turned to Joe. "How about a movie?"

"Okay, *Tio*." The kid smiled at him like he was humoring him. Man, he loved that kid. To him,

War was just "War" and Adam was "Uncle Adam", but he was *"Tio"* and that was special. He didn't get to see his blood nephews and nieces as often as he would've liked. It was nice to have a little buddy around to call him *"Tio"*.

"Pick one out, and I'll make us some popcorn."

By the time he came back to the living room with their midnight snack, Joe had already picked a superhero movie to watch. He wasn't surprised.

Hours later, he woke up to new aches and pains. His ankles hurt from being crossed and propped up on the coffee table. His neck hurt from holding it a certain way. His back hurt from sleeping while sitting up and his head was beginning to throb from lack of a real pillow.

He looked over at Joe curled up on the couch next to him, happily asleep. Then he realized what had woken him up wasn't the migraine he could feel coming on or any of the other pains from falling asleep on the couch, but noises in the kitchen.

The rational, civilian side of his brain said it was probably War or Adam grabbing a late night or early morning snack. Whatever time it was. But the ever-present Devil Dog in the back of his mind was simultaneously cataloging which weapons were where in the house, what he could use if he couldn't get to those, who might be in the kitchen instead of his roommates, and the best way to neutralize the supposed threat without bringing harm to anyone else in the house. Namely, the ten-year-old sleeping on the couch. They'd just celebrated his birthday and his mission in life was to ensure he continued to celebrate those.

As quietly as he could, he rose from the couch and tiptoed to the kitchen. A peek around the corner confirmed it was just War making a sandwich.

"Damn it, man. Don't do that to me."

"Do what?"

"I wake up to strange noises in the middle of the night, and I'm all disoriented from sleeping on the couch. If I were any more messed up in the head, I could have hurt you."

War shrugged. "But you're not." He went back to making his sandwich like nothing could have happened.

That was typical of War, though. Nothing ever seemed to faze him.

They often made jokes about being messed up, but the statement was true. He was one of the lucky ones. His job in the Marine Corps kept him away from some of the more dangerous aspects of war.

He'd experienced a lot, including some messed up shit, but still not nearly as much as some and not as much as he suspected War had experienced. It wasn't a contest, but they wouldn't talk a lot about it, even if it was. He'd lived under the same roof with War and Adam for years and never *really* talked about their military experiences beyond the superficial. That was fine with him, but he hoped if his friends ever needed to talk, they knew he was there for them.

When he realized he'd zoned out for a minute as he stared at the back of War's head, it was to find that War had turned around and was staring back at him with a worried look on his face.

"You all right, man?"

"Of course, I'm all right. I told you. I'm disoriented from being woken up in the middle of the night."

"Okay. Sorry about that. I just got home, and I'm hungry." He looked like he wanted to say more but cut himself off.

"It's all right. I'll see you in the morning." He turned to leave the kitchen and War followed him back to the living room.

"Do you want me to help you blow up the air mattress for your room so you can sleep in your own bed and Joe won't wake up all alone in the living room?"

It was really the last thing he wanted to do—the first was to fall back on the couch and go back to sleep—but he knew the offer was War's olive branch, so he accepted.

War grabbed the mattress and air pump out of the garage while Jesus grabbed a sleeping bag and a pillow out of the hall closet.

They worked in sleepy silence to air up the mattress, and then, as War unzipped the sleeping bag, Jesus went to get Joe. He laid Joe on the sleeping bag, and War zipped him inside.

"There. Like a happy, little soft taco." He laughed at his own joke, but War only cracked a little smile and grunted.

"Shut up, man. I'm still hungry. Your one-man ambush interrupted my dinner."

He almost felt bad about that, but he knew if War was joking about it, then they were cool.

He climbed into bed and crashed out before his head even hit the pillow.

When he woke again, the sun was shining through his window, and the house was completely quiet.

He looked over at the air mattress off to the side of his bed expecting to see Joe still sound asleep, but it was empty.

It must be later than I thought.

He got up and followed his nose into the kitchen. There was no one there, but someone had left him a plate of bacon and eggs. Probably Adam. It was his nature to make sure everyone was taken care of.

He popped the plate in the microwave and added two pieces of bread to the toaster while his coffee brewed in their single serve coffee maker. With his warm plate, toast, and mug, he left the kitchen to search for everyone else.

He found Joe and Adam on the back porch. Adam with a cup of coffee and Joe with his tablet. Heaven forbid that kid go too long without a video game.

He and Adam exchanged half-awake greetings,

while Joe spared him a quick glance and a smile. He'd take what he could get as long as his nose was buried in the tablet.

Someone was missing, though. "Where's War?"

"Asleep still. I guess. I didn't check or anything. Just used the leftover bacon and eggs to make breakfast tacos and threw them in the refrigerator for him for later." Adam had a way of answering his next question before he asked it. His way of avoiding as much small talk as possible.

He set his plate and mug on the patio table and sat down to enjoy his breakfast. It was a quiet, lazy Sunday morning, and it'd been a while since he had one of those. At least, one with the company of anyone else.

Later in the day, after Jesus had already walked Joe home, War appeared looking like he'd barely slept a wink. Again, Jesus wondered if he was going through something he needed to talk about, or maybe he was just burning the candle at both ends. He didn't stick around long enough for Jesus to inquire though.

He heard War's motorcycle leave the garage just as Adam joined him on the living room couch. "I set up some roommate interviews for today. You'll be around, right?"

"Yeah. Until I have to leave for an appointment with a client. What about War?"

"He said he'd be back in time for the first one."

War was back in time for the first candidate, all right. The poor guy, Tom, had just stepped out of his car when War's motorcycle came rumbling around the corner down the street.

Tom went from mildly alarmed to downright pissing himself the closer War got, and he was completely pale by the time War parked his impressive Harley on the sidewalk right next to Tom's sensible sedan.

He froze as he watched War's intimidating stature dismount from his motorcycle, like one wrong move would earn a fist to the face. Not that War would hurt a fly... that didn't deserve it.

Adam cursed under his breath and started down the driveway when he realized Tom was rooted in place with fear. Jesus followed to at least catch the show.

"Tom. Thanks for coming. I see you've met one of my roommates, Warren O'Donnell." Jesus snickered and Adam elbowed him in the ribs. He didn't use his nickname for obvious reasons. "This is my other roommate, Jesus Benavidez. Guys, this is Tom Scott from my office. His lease is up so he just needs a place for a few months before his transfer to our headquarters in Chicago goes through."

"Actually, uh, Adam, uh, I just came by to tell you, in person, that, uh, I found a short-term lease so close to the office that I, uh, just can't pass it up. Thanks, uh, for considering me. I hope I'm, uh, not putting you in a bind."

"Nah, man. Don't worry about us. You seemed pretty insistent yesterday. Are you sure?"

"Yes! Positive." His voice cracked as it came out too loud and panicked.

Jesus would have called him out on the lie if he didn't agree with Tom that he was obviously not a good fit for their spare room.

"Okay bud. If you're sure. We can always come to some kind of agreement about the couch too if your place falls through." Adam was always the helpful, accommodating one.

Tom gave him a genuine smile before remembering to fear the hulking man next to him. "Thanks, Adam. I appreciate your generosity, but I'll be all right. I'll, uh," His eyes flicked to War, then back to Adam. "See you around the office." Adam waved to Tom as he hopped back in his car and drove away.

"That went well." Jesus enjoyed being the sarcastic one. Adam scowled at him and then War and then back at him. War just grunted, but Jesus wasn't as unaffected.

"What did I do?"

"Nothing, Jesus. That's the problem." He gestured to War with a ridged knife hand to show his frustration. "I had War over here being War, and you standing silent. Intimidating. Sentinel. You could've at least smiled and made the guy feel welcome. Instead, it was me and the He-man twins."

"More like He-man and She-ra."

Jesus busted out laughing. War made a joke. Somebody needed to record the moment for the history books. He didn't even care that War called him She-ra. "You're just jealous of my beautiful hair."

Then they were all laughing.

"Why would you even consider that guy, and why wouldn't you at least warn him about his potential roommates?"

"He overheard me on the phone with the guy I'm expecting next, and he practically begged to be considered. He's a great guy, except a little sheltered, and I figured we could put up with anything for a few months if he ended up as the top candidate. Then War comes in as our very own Hell's Angels wannabe."

War grunted his dissention.

"I told him we all met in the Marines, but I guess he pictured three of me, not me plus He-man and She-ra." He smirked. The fucker.

"Okay. I guess we deserve that. Hopefully, the next guy fits in more."

He did, but still wasn't what they were looking for. The kid was about to start his terminal leave and he was young, having only one enlistment under his belt. Too young to share space with the three of them, seasoned as they were. They'd all slowly go insane under the same roof. Jesus was sure that Adam would help the kid find a place more suitable and probably even mentor the kid as he re-entered civilian life, the helpful bastard that he was.

The next guy wasn't due to arrive for another half hour, so Jesus got out his scratch pad to play with a tattoo idea a regular client emailed him about earlier in the day. He didn't usually doodle tattoos in his off time, but it was always fun to work on a new challenge, whether he was on the clock or not.

Not even ten minutes later, though, the doorbell rang. *Damn it.*

He and War made it to the foyer just as Adam was opening the door and greeting the guy standing there.

He was about Adam's height, so a little taller than Jesus, but slimmer than Adam. Slimmer than all of them, but not scrawny. At first, he thought the guy was another young kid, but as he stepped closer, Jesus realized he was closer to thirty than twenty. It was no doubt his strawberry blond hair that gave him a younger look, and the fact that he was dressed like a coed in a hoodie and jeans.

"Hi. I'm BJ. You must be Adam." They shook hands.

"Yes. I am," he replied as he ushered BJ in the door. "And this is Jesus and War. Guys, this is BJ Stratford."

"BJ? Wow. With a name like Blow Job, the alternative must be *really* bad."

"Damn it, Jesus." Three things happened at once. Adam reprimanded him, War chuckled, but BJ full-out laughed.

"Yeah, man. Yeah, it really is. But I'm gonna need at least eight shots of tequila before you ever come close to getting it out of me." He laughed again. "I've heard a lot of Blow Job jokes, but none have hit the nail quite so accurately on the head."

Then Jesus laughed too, and he even got a smile and a half-hearted eyeroll out of Adam.

"So, Beej, you've probably already told Adam a bunch, but tell us about yourself." Unlike the previous two candidates, he cared to learn more about the guy.

"Okay, well, Adam mentioned you're all Marines, so I'll start with 'Corporal Stratford reporting for duty'." He mock-saluted them and they all chuckled, even War.

"I'm originally from Florida but settled here after I got out. I recently became the owner of an auto mechanic shop not too far from here when my friend Henry passed away."

"Henry? As in Henry's Auto Repair?"

"Yeah, that's the one. Are you a customer? Wait, is that your Chevelle in the driveway?"

"Sure is. I was wondering who had taken it over and kept it open. We'll have to talk cars later, so we don't bore the others." He winked at Adam and War. "How about a tour of the house in the meantime?"

"Absolutely. Lead the way."

"War and I will hang back here. It doesn't take three people to show BJ around." Jesus was a little surprised Adam was willing to hang back. Not that it would take long to show an empty bedroom and where everything was. The kitchen was at the end of the tour.

"Any chance you like to cook?" Jesus asked BJ.

"Umm… Not really. Is that a deal breaker? Do y'all take turns cooking or something?"

"Yes. It's a total deal breaker. We're looking for a chef-slash-roommate." He'd spoken deadpan and almost had BJ apologizing before Adam strolled in and ruined his fun.

"Damn it, Jesus. Quit being an ass."

He turned to BJ with a smirk. "Mother Hen here never lets me have any fun."

"He's messing with you. One of our previous roommates handled all the cooking, but we never asked him to pitch in for groceries in exchange. We've been doing okay for ourselves since he moved out." Adam punctuated his statement by smacking Jesus upside the head.

"Hey. Watch the hair."

"Can I ask why that guy moved out?"

"Love." BJ gave him a funny look.

"What Jesus means is he met a girl, and they bought a house down the street."

About that time, Jesus realized they were one man short. "Where's War?"

"He said he made his decision. BJ, I think Jesus will agree with War and me. The room's yours if you want it."

BJ turned to look at Jesus, so he nodded his agreement. "Hell yes. Absolutely. I accept."

Adam and Jesus laughed. "Good. We've already talked about the move-in date and rent amount on the phone, so I'll get you a roommate agreement to sign. It's pretty standard. Don't be a dick to us. We won't be a dick to you. If we get on each other's nerves, we can put on some gloves and take it out on each other in the garage gym."

"Y'all have a gym?"

"Fuck. I forgot the best part of the tour!" Jesus opened the door that led from the kitchen to the garage and flicked on the light.

"Damn. This *is* the best part of the tour."

Jesus chuckled. "I wouldn't have guessed you'd feel that way."

BJ lifted the hem of his hoodie to reveal a well-defined six-pack of abs and smirked. "A body like this takes work."

Jesus bounced his pecs in response and said, "I know."

"Okay, boys. We can play 'Whose is bigger?' later."

They both said, "Mine" at the same time, and Adam rolled his eyes.

Then they heard the front door open as they headed back into the house. "Hello! Where is everybody?"

"Will, what's up, man?" Adam gave him and Joe a fist bump, and Nikki a peck on the cheek. Jesus followed up with hugs all around.

"War called and said I should 'walk my happy ass down here and meet my replacement'." They all laughed.

He held out his hand to the new guy. "Hey man. I'm Will. I hear you'll be taking over my old room."

"BJ. So you're the chef I have to live up to."

"Guilty. And this is my fiancé, Nikki, and our son, Joe."

"Nice to meet y'all."

"Well, I hate to break up the love fest, but I've gotta get to the studio. Nice to meet you, Beej. I hope it works out with you. Let me know if you need any help moving."

"It's BJ."

"Yeah… I can't call you that."

That earned him another eye roll from Adam, a sigh from Will and a grin from BJ. At least someone got it. Funny, it was the same guy he was hazing.

Chapter Six

Stacey

Distant chiming bells woke her from sleep, such as it was, and she listened to them crescendo louder and louder as she felt around her nightstand. Opening her eyes would require more energy than she was willing to expel until she knew who was calling.

Finally capturing the noisy offender, she peeked at the screen and rolled her eyes before she accepted the call and brought it to her ear. This should be good.

"Hey, Aunt Brenda. What's up?"

"Hey, Sugar Pie. Did I wake you?"

"It's early on a Sunday morning and I only got off work a few hours ago. You know you did." She laughed at her aunt's fake innocent act. "The question is 'Why?'."

"Okay. Okay. The bartender I hired for my party tonight just canceled on me. Any chance…?"

She groaned as she rolled over and sat up on the edge of the bed.

"Geez, girl. You sound twice, no, make that trice your age. What do you have to groan about?" She gasped. "Oh! Did I interrupt something? Please tell me I interrupted something. It's been a while since you got laid."

"Damn, Aunt Brenda. It's too early for that shit, and who says 'trice' anymore?" She laughed at her aunt again. It was nothing new from her, and yet she loved her; crazy, meddling ways and all. "Do you need my help, or do you want some more time to call me a dried-up twenty-something?"

"Don't be daft." She tsked. "I can do both! But dear, you are not dried-up. You just act like it." Her aunt cackled, and she tried to keep a straight face but failed.

Refusing to discuss her love life any further with her aunt, she changed the subject. "First 'trice' and now 'daft'? Are you reading Regency Romance books again?"

"No. Nothing like that. I met a man! He's a stage actor and loves using words no one uses anymore. He's got me spouting all kinds of shit." Stacey snorted. "If you come tonight, you'll get to meet him. So, can you? Or are you working at the bar tonight?"

She thought for a moment and let the silence stretch out between them. Even if she'd had to call into work, she'd do whatever her aunt needed, but if she agreed too fast, her aunt would accuse her of having no social life. She didn't have one, technically, but the dance kept her from having to talk about it.

"What time do you need me?"

"Oh, six or so. Seven would even be okay. I can set everything up and all you have to do is serve if you can't get here until then. The party won't even really get going until eight or nine."

She huffed. "Okay, Aunt Brenda. I'll do it. I have to work today, but I should be able to get there by seven. I'm sure you can handle any early birds before I arrive. You did teach me everything I know." Well, nearly everything. She'd picked up some more difficult recipes and techniques since she started working at Kelly's, but she wouldn't need any of that working for her aunt. Her aunt's friends were old school and easy to please.

They were also hilarious. She gave her aunt a hard time about helping her out, but really, she enjoyed her time with the colorful group of artists. They'd all gotten her through the hardest time of her life after she'd left home a disgraced mess and taken refuge with her aunt as a teenager.

Out of the bubble she'd grown up in, she'd learned quickly that not everyone saw the world the narrow way her parents and their church did. That her error did not make her a bad person, and it was possible to put it behind her. To move on and not let the blunder, as big as it had been, define her future.

Not yet an adult, but pushed out into the world anyway, her aunt and her aunt's friends had finished raising her when her parents gave up. They'd given her the love and guidance she'd needed. She was forever indebted to them but knew she'd never be able to truly repay them.

When Stacey first came to San Diego from Houston, she would shut herself in her room during the parties or go out and find her own fun. Her aunt always assured her she was welcome to join, but it was months and numerous parties later before she felt comfortable enough to join the festivities. It wasn't long before her aunt's welcoming friends pulled her out of her shell and became like surrogate aunts and uncles. Thanks to them, she felt like she went from having no one to having an extended family bigger than ever before. She hadn't seen everyone in a while. It would be good to catch up with them all.

After hanging up with her aunt and unable to go back to sleep, she shuffled to the kitchen and started some coffee. She was going to need a lot of it to make it through the day.

Slow, even by Sunday standards, she was able to leave the pub early and make it to her aunt's condo with plenty of time to help the caterers set up the bar. It wouldn't be a large party, but her aunt always pulled out all the stops for her get-togethers.

As her aunt's guests began arriving, each one was surprised and excited to see Stacey behind the bar, and she was just as excited to see them. It was nice to catch up with the people who'd helped her find her footing when it'd felt like her life was in shambles and she'd never be able to put the pieces back together. She didn't have the career she once thought she'd have or even gone to college like she thought she would, but she also wasn't the girl she once was either. That girl was weak and naïve, and Stacey vowed to never be either one of those things again.

When her aunt's new beau, Jack, came through the door, Brenda dragged the poor man straight to the bar for introductions. He was a tall, thin man with a friendly face and prominent laugh-lines who seemed just as enamored with her aunt as her aunt was with him. He did have a funny way of saying some things, but he also spoke how you would expect a stage actor who specialized in Shakespeare to speak. In riddles and old English.

As the night progressed, many of the guests congregated around the bar "catching up", which consisted of grilling her about her love life. When she mentioned taking the job at the tattoo studio, her aunt's friend, Diana, asked if that meant she would be working with hot tattoo artists.

To her horror, Stacey could feel her face heat up. "Oh, she's blushing. Tell us about him, or them. Is there more than one hottie?"

Before she could think too hard about Diana, a

woman in her fifties, using the word "hottie", her aunt spoke up. "Tell them about the beefcake who got you the job."

"He didn't *get* me the job." *And I never told you what he looked like.*

"So, you agree he's a beefcake." Diana threw her an overexaggerated wink at the end of her statement.

She snorted. "More like beef-y." She tried to lie believably.

Diana just shrugged. "That's okay. Usually thick men also have nice, thick…"

"Dear God, Diana." She interrupted. "Make it stop. I'll give anything for you not to complete that sentence."

"Anything?" Brenda raised her eyebrows with the question.

"What could you possibly want? I'm already giving you bartending."

"Yeah, because I can't get you to come otherwise."

Stacey just stared at her aunt for a moment. "You never hired anyone else, did you?"

"Nope." Not an ounce of shame.

"Then why did you wait until the last minute to call me? I could've been busy." That was another lie, but her aunt had the good grace not to call her on it.

"It had to be believable that I was in a bind."

"You never even had bartenders at your parties before you taught me the basics."

Why am I just now thinking of that?

"Yeah, like savages." Diana, always so helpful when she spoke up.

"So, sue me. I wanted to give you a reason to come over just like back when I wanted you to come out of your room, and everyone's been asking about you."

Had she been that neglectful of spending time with some of the most important people in her life? "I'm sorry, Aunt Brenda." She came around the bar and hugged the woman who'd saved her when everyone else gave up and helped her put the pieces of herself back together.

"That's okay, dear. Make it up to me by telling us about that beefy beefcake."

She rolled her eyes and groaned. "There's nothing to tell. He's cute." More like Hot with a capital H. "But he's such a player and a flirt. He reminds me too much of you-know-who, and I just don't want to go down that road again. Plus, the owner has a rule against dating coworkers."

"Who said anything about dating?" Diana again with her helpfulness, wagging her eyebrows.

"I understand why you're wary, Stacey, but don't close yourself off from something good because of all the 'what-ifs'." Her aunt had been telling her that in one way or another since she'd come to live with her.

"Yeah, you're young. Act like it. Sounds like this beefcake would be perfect for some no-strings-attached fun, if you know what I mean." Everyone within earshot knew what Diana meant.

Could she, though? No. Probably not. That wasn't her style. At least, it wasn't her style anymore. Her very first experience with sex had made her think and overthink every sexual encounter since. She either got drunk enough to throw caution to the wind, or she weighed every possible outcome *ad nauseum* until she talked herself out of it. Her relationships—if you could even call them that—all either didn't make it to sex or didn't last much longer past it. What made it worse was she was never comfortable enough with any of them to confess why she was having a hard time. Maybe she *was* going about it all wrong. Maybe she needed someone who could help her turn her brain off.

"I know that look." Diana gave her a conspiratorial look. "She's thinking about it."

"Shut up." Because Stacey was *so* grown-up.

Diana and Brenda cackled like hens at her expense.

Chapter Seven

Jesus

On Tuesday, he arrived at the studio before anyone else again and entered the back door with a spring in his step. The door closed and locked again behind him, and that made him wonder if Jeff gave Stacey her own code to gain access to the building yet.

The front door was a simple deadbolt because they usually locked and unlocked it from the inside, but each person who worked there had their own code for the back door. The computerized lock recorded who entered and when and stored that information for retrieval for up to a year.

He went to the breakroom and started a pot of coffee. It may have been almost two o'clock in the afternoon, but he was still about to put in a full day's work, and that required a few cups of coffee. While the pot brewed, he went to his station and started getting it ready. He didn't have a scheduled client for a few hours, but he always liked to be as ready as possible for any walk-in's he could squeeze into his schedule.

He heard the back door open and looked up to see Jeff walk through the door. They nodded in greeting to each other as Jeff went straight to his office. His head popped up again as Derrick and then Troy, both resident tattoo artists, walked through the door, and he was beginning to get whiplash.

He heard the door open again and was tempted not to look but knew it could only be Stacey. He caught her eye and smiled. She smiled back.

He was in serious trouble, or maybe she was, if she couldn't even walk into a room without him noticing. He'd have to get over that or working with her would wreak havoc on his sanity. His mind was supposed to be on his work when his clients were in his chair.

"Hey, Stacey. I see Jeff filled you in on the deal with the back door. He's in his office if you need to see him, and if he's not around later, feel free to ask me if you need anything."

She just nodded at him and turned the direction of Jeff's office.

Ugh. He was trying too hard and probably came off creepy to her. He felt dumb. He'd have to combat that feeling by ignoring her until she had a reason to talk to him. No way in Hell could he be the one to speak next. It was her turn. And he was a thirteen-year-old boy in junior high learning how to talk to girls again.

He stifled the urge to bang his head against the wall and focused on the rest of his station set-up.

He could be so smooth when he didn't really care what a girl thought of him, but he'd never felt as uncool as he did when Stacey was around. There was just something about her that affected him differently than any girl had in a long time. Like her opinion of him mattered when normally he couldn't give half a shit.

He went back to the breakroom to grab a cup of the coffee he'd brewed and found Jeff introducing Stacey to the remaining two artists that she hadn't already met.

"Stacey, these guys are Derrick and Troy. Guys, this is Stacey, our new studio manager."

"Hi Stacey, nice to meet you." Derrick spoke up and shook her hand while Troy just nodded and waved with two fingers. Anyone else, he would have considered the gesture to be sarcastic, but he was never sure what was going on in Troy's head. He wasn't exactly rude or condescending, but maybe "aloof" was the right word. In truth, Jesus didn't know either of their newest artists well. They'd been with the studio for a while but not as long as Dillon and Beau, and neither seemed to want to make friends with anyone, including each other.

"Jesus." He looked up from the counter where he'd been making his coffee when Jeff called his name. "I want Erik to sit with you during the last session of that back-piece you're doing today. Let him try his hand at it if you're comfortable, but no worries if you're not. I already talked to the client, so he knows what to expect." He turned back to Stacey. "I'll introduce Erik when he gets here. He's our apprentice."

They'd already spoken about this, or he would've been pretty peeved that Jeff had taken it upon himself to contact his client. He took pride in the relationships he'd cultivated with his repeat clients, and owner or not, they were his, not Jeff's. Luckily, this man had been a client of his for years and knew Jeff well enough, too. He was an easy-going guy and therefore the perfect opportunity for real-life practice for their apprentice.

After being hunched over his client for hours, he stood and arched his back to get the kinks out.

"Jesus, this came out sick." His long-time client, Kris, turned back and forth in front of the mirror to see the entire back piece that had taken three sessions to finish.

He chuckled. "I'm glad you like it."

"Hell yeah, and I can't even tell which parts the kid inked. You better watch it; he's going to be stealing your clients before too long."

"Trying to tell me something, man?"

Kris laughed. "Nah. You're stuck with me."

"Good." Jesus sighed. "I'm not really worried. Kid's got talent. He should use it, and there's plenty of work to go around. I've got the back aches to prove it."

They laughed.

"Do you want me to take a picture of it before I cover it?"

"Yeah. Would you?" Kris handed Jesus his phone.

He snapped a few photos before handing the phone back and covering the new tattoo so Kris could put his shirt back on.

Walking up to the front desk with Kris, he took a moment to check on Stacey while she took Kris's credit card, swiped it and offered him aftercare instructions. As the one who'd told her about the job, he felt a sense of responsibility to make sure she was getting along okay. That was totally the *only* reason he thought about her wellbeing. She seemed tired, but not too stressed out. Not bad for her first day.

As a regular client, Kris declined the instructions that he already knew by heart and bid them goodnight before heading out the door.

Jeff had stuck around and actually trained Stacey, which was more than the last shop manager got. Of course, the last manager was a man, and Jeff was always more hands-on with the female managers. Not to the point of creepiness or being over-the-line, but they definitely received more of his attention.

"So, you want to start sweeping in the front or the back?" They were the last two at the studio, so it was their job to clean and close the place down.

"I don't know, the front, I guess. Why?"

"I figure you start at one end, I'll start at the

other, and we'll meet in the middle."

"Why?"

"It gets done faster that way."

"No. Why are you helping?"

"Because I always help."

She raised an eyebrow at him like she didn't believe him. Difficult woman. "The last artist always helps the manager close. Hell, we have to close by ourselves when you're not here anyway. At least it goes faster with two people. Or it would've if you hadn't picked an argument and we'd just gotten it done."

She huffed, walked to the supply closet, grabbed two brooms, and shoved one at him before walking to the front of the store to start sweeping. It wasn't until she stopped and looked at him like he was dumb before he uprooted his feet from the spot by the desk and went to the back of the studio to start sweeping his own section.

They finished the remainder of the closing procedures in awkward near silence, only speaking when necessary, and said quick goodbyes as they parted ways at the back door before walking to their respective cars.

Jesus knew one thing for sure, they wouldn't be able to continue like that, alternating back and forth between tiptoeing around each other and picking arguments.

But weeks passed, and the only thing that changed was the seasons. Spring fell away into summer, and while they only closed together a couple of times each week, their interactions were either awkward or combative. The mixed signals were making his head spin. He couldn't tell if she wanted to slap him or screw him most of the time. Not that he wished for the days when she hated him for no reason, but at least then he knew where they stood.

On the other hand, she was warming up to him. Sort of. Gradually. At least until she realized she was. Then she would tense up and get prickly all over again, like she was fighting her own internal battle against liking him. But he was finding that busting through the ice was getting just a little easier each time they interacted.

As far as her job as manager was concerned, she was kick-ass. She organized the studio and the fuckers in it, and just like at the bar, she did it with a smile on her face for everyone but him. He got the occasional smirk out of her, but she always recovered quickly with a deliberate frown. They were small wins, but wins, nonetheless.

On a Friday, they walked into the studio within minutes of each other and he knew it was going to be a good day if they were both closing again. He was determined to reach some sort of truce with her. The occasional glimpses he got of the easy-going girl she could be were not enough. He was selfish. He wanted her to be like that with him all the time, not just when she accidentally left her guard down.

While measuring out coffee grounds for the coffee machine, she came up beside him at the counter. "Why don't you let me do that so you can set up your station?"

"Thanks, but I've got it. I don't have a client for a little while, and even if I did, they would have to wait until I've had my coffee." He turned to wink at her as they both reached for the handle of the coffee pot but forgot about the wink when their hands touched and their eyes locked. There was a gasp. Had she done that, or was it him? It was like someone had sucked the air out of the room and deprived his brain of oxygen.

All he could think about was the fact that he'd never touched her hand before that moment, or he would have definitely remembered it. As if he'd been electrocuted, his muscles locked, and his brain disconnected from his extremities.

"Oh good, you're both here." Troy's entrance shattered the moment they'd been frozen in, and they both rushed to pull their hands away from the coffeepot handle. "I know we're all closing tonight, but I have somewhere I need to be, so do you mind if I head out and make it up to you next time?"

He answered absentmindedly, "Yeah. Yeah, sure." Then he paused and chanced a glance at Stacey. "I mean, if that's okay with the shop manager."

"What? Oh. Yeah. It's fine. It's not a three-person job anyway." She smiled at Troy, but it didn't reach her eyes. She was still just as dazed as Jesus was. What the hell had just happened between them?

She hustled out of the room to wherever to do something while he finished making the coffee before retreating back to the sanctity of his own station.

Completely distracted all day, it was a wonder he didn't screw up any tattoos, but somehow, he made it to the end of the day.

Once again, they were the last two people in the studio, left alone to close everything up.

Stacey went to the supply room and grabbed two brooms. She didn't even spare him a glance as she gave one to him on her way to the front of the store. That wasn't what he wanted, though. Before she could remove her hand from the broom that she'd passed to him, he grabbed her and the broom and pulled her toward him.

Her shocked eyes looked up at him as she attempted to pull back. "What are you doing?"

"I'm not really sure. I just know that I can't go another moment until I figure out what's going on."

She stopped trying to pull out of his grasp. "Huh? Going on with what?"

"With you. With me. I can't seem to do anything right around you, but I can't seem to stop trying, either. I've never been so upside down and inside out in my life. What is it about you?"

"Hmm. My ass? My hair? My boobs? Pick one or all of the above. It's all men ever see about me, but in the end, does it matter? The outcome is the same."

He smirked at her. "Oh, yeah? What's that?"

She stood on her tiptoes and whispered in his ear. "Blue balls."

He threw his head back and laughed as she renewed her struggle to pull back from him. This time, he let her. She walked to the front of the shop to start sweeping, but he set his broom aside and followed. "Let me tell you a secret, *mariposa*. You never leave me with blue balls." She looked up at him as he stalked closer and stood still as he leaned down to whisper back in her ear. "Even in my mind, you always get the job done."

She pushed him back. "Ugh. Men are pigs." Her words said one thing, but the smirk on her lips and color on her cheeks told him she enjoyed hearing him say that. He got closer again and when she wouldn't look at him, he used his hand to tip her chin up. "I bet if I unbuttoned those tight jeans of yours and stuck my hand in your underwear, I'd find your cunt all wet for me. Wouldn't I?"

She shook her head.

"No? Why not, *mariposa*?"

She bit her lip. "Joke's on you. I'm not wearing any underwear."

He nearly swallowed his tongue and the rush of blood to his cock made him lightheaded when she let her broom drop to the floor and moved his hand to the button on her pants. He looked in her eyes to see if she was serious before he hit the light and pulled her by the waistband of her jeans to his station.

The only lighting was from the emergency lights, but it was enough to see what he was doing. He spun her around and bent her over his tattoo bench where his clients usually sat, lined his cock up with the seam of her ass and was unbuttoning her pants when she placed a hand over his to stop him. "What about the cameras?"

"They don't reach back here for the privacy of our clients." He went back to work on her zipper when she stilled him again.

"You'll have to sanitize your bench again."

"Worth it." He went back to work, but then stopped himself. "And, before you ask or have another objection, I have a condom, too. Anything else?"

She stilled, and he worried she was going to call it off or that he'd misread what she wanted. He'd do whatever she wanted, but damn, he hoped she wanted what he did.

His answer came when she rubbed her ass against his dick. "If you stop now, I'll never forgive you." There was a weight to her words that he didn't stop to examine too hard.

He just chuckled and resumed getting her pants open. "Yes, ma'am."

He finished pushing her zipper down and

stepped back to peel the tight jeans down her thighs. She moved as if to push them down and off, but he stopped her. He wanted them tight around her calves. With her exposed ass in the air and her pussy peeking out between her thighs, he took a moment to admire the sight in what little light he had.

Her movements to stand up, though, obstructed his view, so he crowded her against the bench and leaned her back over it, blanketing her smaller frame with his large body. Finding her hands, he brought them up to grip the edge of the bench. When he was sure she would keep them there, he stood slowly as he ran both hands down her back. He left one on the small of her back as he tapped her ass cheek and then plunged two fingers into her cunt with the other hand.

She jerked under his hand from the spanking, but her curses died in a moan from the intrusion, and her gushing pussy told him she loved every minute. He stroked in and out as she got wetter and wetter. He began to spread her juices to her clit, circling it, pinching it and rubbing it as it swelled. He crouched down and added his tongue, fucking her with it while his fingers focused on her clit. He licked upward to her ass as he plunged his thumb into her cunt and pinched her clit with his fingers. She squirmed and bucked as he held her by her cunt and circled her pink rosebud with his tongue before slipping it in her clinched hole. There was no way she was ready to be fucked in the ass, but ass-play was his favorite, whether it resulted in anal or not.

"Oh God. I'm so close. Jesus!"

He smiled against her ass. He loved when women cursed his name. With one hand, he plunged two fingers in her pussy and one in her ass, while speeding up his fingers on her clit with his other hand. "Come for me, *mariposa*."

She screamed, and he smiled to himself, thinking that the cameras wouldn't pick up any video of their encounter, but they definitely heard that scream.

She groaned when he removed his hands from her, but it was only long enough to undo his pants, put the condom on, grab her hips and place his cock at her entrance. "You still want this, *mariposa*?"

She pushed back, and he thought he saw her nod. "It's dark in here, sweetheart, and I can't hear your head rattle. I need words."

"Yes. Fuck me, please Jesus. Do it. Do it now."

They both moaned as he pushed inside her. Damn, it was like heaven. No woman had any right to feel that good. She was tight, oh so tight, as he started to move back and forth. So tight, it was almost like she was...

He stopped. *Fuck.* "You're not a virgin, are you?"

She laughed. Not just a chuckle, but a full-blown belly laugh. If he wasn't freaking out, he would have enjoyed the clinching that happened around his dick as she laughed her head off.

He was about to ask her what the fuck was so funny when she answered. "No. I'm not. It's just been a little while."

The tension left his shoulders and he let his head hang down to stare at her heart-shaped ass pressed up against his hips. "Thank fuck."

He resumed pushing and pulling, faster and harder, until they were both grunting and out of breath. At first, she was meeting him thrust for thrust until her movement began to falter.

"Almost there. More."

He loosened her grip on the edge of the bench and brought her hands behind her back, where he grabbed her by the wrists, pulling her towards him as he pushed into her. "Let me handle it, *mariposa*. You just feel."

"Oh, God. Oh, God. Jesus. Oh, God."

"That's right, *mariposa*. Let go. Damn, you're so beautiful. Let me see you come again. I want to feel you clamp down on my cock."

While keeping his punishing rhythm, he moved both wrists to one hand as he reached around and played with her clit again until she exploded in her second orgasm, sending him over the edge with her as he bent over her body on the bench and came stronger than he could ever remember.

When their orgasms and all the aftershocks had passed, he sat up and pulled out gingerly. He threw the condom away and grabbed the pack of baby wipes he kept at his station. Pulling one out for each of them, he debated whether he should wipe her down or let her do it, but she decided for him when she sat up and took it from him.

They cleaned up and fixed their clothes, and before he could figure out what to say, she kissed his cheek and left. He had barely enough time to get his brain in gear and follow her to the door so he could at least make sure she made it to her car and drove away okay. Some long-ago extinct caveman in him demanded he follow her home and make sure she made it in her door okay too, but he told that guy to fuck off because that would certainly freak her out.

It wasn't until he was sweeping the entire shop by himself and re-sanitizing his bench that he lamented he didn't even get to kiss her. Somewhere along the way, he'd completely skipped that step and nearly all of the other steps that most people consider important before fucking someone, but he never cared before. He wasn't starting now.

Chapter Eight

Stacey

Damn him. Damn them. Damn me. It'd been good. It'd been great. It'd been the best sex of her life, and she couldn't stop thinking about it. He'd taken control and for the first time ever, her mind completely blanked, and she just felt. She felt him guide her to his station and felt him bend her over the bench. She felt the rigidness of his cock against her ass as he blanketed her body and silently commanded her to grip the edge for dear life. She felt his tongue and fingers penetrating the most intimate parts of her and the wicked things that no man had ever done before. She felt the size of him as he finally pushed into her, the grip on her wrists as he pulled her to him, impaling her over and over, and the bite of the bench against her thighs as he relentlessly pounded her into it.

Reliving it over and over in her mind for days, there wasn't much room for anything else. She had to ask tattoo clients to repeat appointment requests and pub patrons to repeat their drink orders. She avoided Jesus when she could, but when she couldn't, it was like she was a Tesla coil, sending out streamer arcs of electricity whenever he was around. She was amazed she couldn't actually see the lightning dancing back and forth between them.

Sex was supposed to get him out of her system—a hate-fuck to end all—but instead he'd completely fried her system. Her body screamed out to him, and her hormones resonated with him, but her mind knew it'd been a mistake. A stupid, stupid mistake. Doing it again and letting him even farther under her skin would be an even worse mistake. She was better than that. She was stronger than that. She had to be, or she was in big trouble.

While she just wanted to pretend it didn't happen, she could tell he wanted to bring it up, but held back out of respect to her unspoken wishes or whatever. Whether he wanted to clear the air or do it again, she didn't know, but she knew that she just wanted to move on and forget about it. That was what she told herself anyway. She had her doubts that she'd be able to ever forget, but she knew she could pretend like she had. She had plenty of experience with pretending like she was okay when she was far from it.

Reminding herself that she was just a way of fulfilling a *need* to him, and how he'd betrayed his own friend for those *needs* was the only way she kept herself from throwing herself at him and begging for a repeat. He probably didn't even want a repeat anyway. Doubtful that he even did repeats, she convinced herself he just wanted to hit it and quit it. There was no way he'd been as affected by that night as she was. Just no way. He was a player. He had great sex all the time. She was nothing special, just a hole to stick it in. She shuddered at the thought, as her mind became more and more disgusted by her own actions and her hormones just screamed out for more.

Avoiding Aunt Brenda's calls was a must too. There was no way she'd get more than five words into a conversation with her intuitive aunt without being called out for hiding something. Then she'd spill everything. She didn't want her aunt to commiserate with her or congratulate her and tell her to move on to the next hunk in line. *Like there are so many.* She felt like she'd reverted to the reckless teenager she turned into when she first came to San Diego, and she needed to understand how she felt about that before muddling her mind with other people's *strong* opinions.

As busy as the studio was, it'd been easy to avoid speaking directly to Jesus or winding up alone in a room with him where he could spark a conversation with her, but the universe decided a week was all she got before it threw them back together again. Once she'd swept up and realized he was still with a client, she could've left him alone to close up, but awkward or not, she wasn't that kind of person. So, she sat down on the couch in the waiting area while he finished up and exhaustion claimed her.

Warm hands cupped her face just before she felt the press of lips against hers. She didn't have to open her eyes to know who was kissing her. His scent was unmistakable, and his lips were as soft as they looked. Slow and sensuous, he brought her out of a hazy dreamland and into a dream-like reality. A small moan escaped her lips as his tongue slipped in to find hers.

Slowly, like their minds were connected, they laid on the couch with her back to the cushions and him on top between her legs. She took the opportunity to wrap her legs around him and extinguish any air left between their bodies. He growled and deepened the kiss.

"Stacey."

How is he talking and kissing at the same time?

"Mariposa." *She secretly loved when he called her that, but he needed to shut up and focus on kissing her.*

"Rise and shine, *mariposa*."

Wait. What?

Chapter Nine

Jesus

He'd tried speaking to her all weekend, but she ran from him at every chance. Frustrated, he just wanted to know that they were okay, that she was okay. She didn't strike him as the kind of girl that, well… did that with just anyone. Whatever she was feeling, though, he was sure that she still didn't think highly of him, and he was no closer to finding out why she had such a low opinion of him.

The shop was closed on Mondays, and he miraculously had Tuesday and Wednesday off, so it was Thursday before he saw her again. But on both Thursday and Friday, she opened, and he closed, so even then, it was only for a few hours in passing between a couple of walk-ins.

It was nearly midnight on Saturday when he finished up with his last client. The appointment had taken longer than he'd anticipated because she had him tweak the design repeatedly. He wanted to get frustrated with her, but he knew how important it was for her to be happy with it. It was, after all, going to be permanently inked on her body, barring some very expensive and painful procedures to remove it.

It wasn't until he was done and walking his client and her husband to the door that he realized Stacey was still there.

She was sitting on the couch in the waiting area. Her elbow was on the arm, her head was propped up on her hand, and she was fast asleep.

He almost didn't want to wake her, but he needed to lock up and they both needed to head home. To their own homes. Individually. Damn. He needed to get his head out of the gutter.

"Stacey." Nothing.

He shook her shoulder a little. "*Mariposa.*" Nothing.

He knelt down in front of her and spoke a little louder as he shook her shoulder again. "Rise and shine, *mariposa.*"

"Hmm?" She stirred but didn't fully wake.

"Time to wake up." She finally woke up with a start when he touched her shoulder.

"Oh crap. I can't believe I fell asleep." *Is she blushing?*

"What are you still doing here?" Damn, if he'd known she was still there, finishing that last tattoo while knowing they were the last two in the studio besides his clients would've been next to impossible.

She shrugged. "I thought it was cruel to leave you here by yourself. The rule at the bar is no one locks up alone."

"Well, this isn't the bar and one of the artists almost always locks up alone when you're not here. We're a small shop. That's just how it is." He thought it was adorable that she was worried about his safety. He was a trained Marine, and she was maybe one-hundred-forty pounds soaking wet. With a perfect hourglass figure and great thighs that he'd like to...

"I realize that, but just because something has always been done a certain way doesn't mean it has to continue to be that way. As long as I'm here, if I see that someone is going to be closing by themselves, I'm going to stay with them."

He admired that about her. Not just her ethics about leaving someone behind, but that she was already putting her mark on the place.

"You're right. It's a good idea, and I will do the same."

She smiled at him like he surprised her. "Uh, thanks. Not sure how Jeff will feel about it, but I believe it's a good policy."

"He'll be on board. Looks like you already swept up. Thanks for that. Gather your things and give me a minute to wipe down my station. Then I'll walk you to your car."

They met at the back door, and he opened it for her. As she brushed by, her scent enveloped him in a cloud of flowers and fruit, and the hairs on his arms rose at her proximity.

Every time he was close to her, he had to resist

the urge to reach out and pull her into his arms, where he knew she felt so right against him. He questioned where the foreign feelings were coming from, and mildly worried whether there was something wrong with him. Like maybe his hormones were off. He wasn't usually so drawn to a woman or clingy after he'd already been with her, especially not when she barely tolerated his existence.

He walked her to her car as he said he would, and when she unlocked it with her key fob, he took the opportunity to open her door for her, too.

"Such a gentleman. Sometimes." She smiled, so he knew she was teasing. "Just wish I could tell when it was genuine."

That threw him off. "What do you mean?"

"You know."

"No. I don't."

They stood there for a moment with the door in between them. Her about to get in the car. Him about to shut the door once she was seated.

"You're going to make me spell it out?"

"Yes. Apparently, I'm too dense to figure it out for myself."

"Apparently."

She paused again, and he was getting a little impatient, waiting for a response.

"Well. Out with it." He must've succeeded in keeping the agitation out of his voice. Otherwise, she probably wouldn't have continued.

"You're so smooth all the time. I used to think

it was never genuine, but now I know you can be a truly nice guy. But now I can't tell the difference between smooth-wants-to-get-in-my-pants-again-Jesus and friendly-sincere-nice-guy-Jesus."

As disconcerting as it was to hear it from her, he had to laugh because it wasn't the first time that he'd heard something similar.

He leaned in a little closer. "Can I let you in on a secret?"

She just nodded.

"You can't tell the difference because there is no difference. I hate to break it to you, *mariposa*, but I'm just friendly. Some have even called me charming, but I only use my powers for good."

He smirked, and she scoffed. "Yeah, right. You charm plenty of girls right out of their panties with no regard for the consequences, including me."

That actually caught him off-guard. She was good at that. But he knew she was wrong.

"I hope you have an explanation for that statement, because I promise you, I'm very aware of the consequences of sex, and while there are no guarantees, I'm not overly cavalier when it comes to safe sex. You of all people know that. And when I want something, I take it. I don't need to charm or trick a girl into bed. She knows what I want the moment our eyes meet, and if she's into it, there's very little talking needed. You should already know that as well. I gave you plenty of chances to say no that night, and if you had, I would've backed off. No question."

She shivered, and he realized that despite the door in between them, he'd gotten so close to her that their noses were almost touching. "That's not what I'm talking about."

"Then what are you talking about, *mariposa*? Just because I can read your body like a second-grade textbook doesn't mean I can read your mind."

Then she said something, but her whisper was so small he couldn't make out her words. "What?"

She took a deep breath and spoke louder, though not much. "Then what about that night you left the bar with Nikki?"

"Huh? What night?" It took a moment to jog his memory of the night he ran into Nikki at Kelly's when he convinced her to give Will another chance. If he were in a laughing mood, he'd think it was hilarious that Stacey thought he slept with Nikki, when all they talked about was his roommate. "You think I... You think we...? No. Hell. No. I just walked her to her car. How did you even hear about that? You didn't work there back then. Did you?

"I would never, could never, do that to a friend, much less a brother. I grew up with all sisters, but I found my brothers in the Marines. Well, and some more sisters, too. I could never betray one of them like that. I could never be that person, period. I know I get more than my fair share of tail, but they're all single as far as I know. Damn, Stacey. What the Hell did I ever do to you for you to think so little of me?"

She froze. He froze. He'd done it. He'd asked the million-dollar question. The one he'd been dying to know for so long. And he'd just spit it out in the heat of the moment.

Chapter Ten

Stacey

Shit on a shingle. She was an idiot. She had thought the worst of him for no other reasons than his flirty personality, her jaded view of men, and a story told by a pathological liar. She knew she could be a bitter bitch, but at that moment, she was embarrassed she'd let it go on for so long without figuring out the truth.

She had nothing to say. No good comeback. No simple explanation. Just like everything else in her life up to that point, it was complicated.

She jumped in the car and shut the door so quickly; she surprised both of them. Before he could react, she was gone; out of the parking lot and headed for home. Her safe space.

So not only was she an idiot, but a coward as well. Gee. If her parents could see her now. They'd be so proud.

Oh well. At least they weren't around for her to disappoint anymore. Their choice. Not hers. It had taken her years to see it, they did her a favor when they disowned her. Years had passed since she'd seen or spoken to them last.

She came screeching into her apartment complex like Jesus was chasing her and rushed into her apartment. Shutting the door, she leaned against the back of it and so many emotions hit her at once that she felt like crying, just to release one or two.

Instead, she grabbed a bottle of wine and retreated to the only place that ever made her feel better.

She leaned over the side of the tub and placed the stopper over the drain. As the tub filled, she tossed in some bath salts and oils that were supposed to be calming and relaxing. Striping out of her clothes, she climbed in before the water was warm enough to dissolve the salts completely. Normally, she would have waited before plopping in, but she just wanted to get to soaking and drinking as fast as possible.

Willing herself to relax, she sat back in the warming bath as the water rose around her and took a gulp straight from the bottle. She'd made an ass of herself. She wondered how she missed the mark so badly... again. Years ago, she believed the best in someone and got burned. This time she believed the worst in someone, and she was still the one who looked like a fool.

Seven years ago

As she laid in the hospital bed, she looked down at the bundle in her arms through tearful eyes. Maybe it was the rush of hormones you get after giving birth, but she wasn't mad or sad, or even happy. She wasn't any of those things because she was all those things and more. She was so happy for the beautiful baby girl in her arms and thankful there were no complications during delivery. She was angry she'd been completely alone. No parents, no friends, not even the baby's father, but he was the first to bail. Her parents were next. They thought kicking her out would teach her a lesson, but by then, the lesson was already growing in her belly. Her friends were last and probably the biggest shock of all. The ones who didn't call her a whore to her face called her one behind her back, and everyone pretended she didn't exist once she transferred to the accelerated high school to graduate before she gave birth.

Mostly, though, she was sad that this would be her only contact with the baby for the foreseeable future.

Sure, she'd picked out amazing adoptive parents for her baby girl, and Ross and Linda promised to send photos over the years, but they all agreed on no contact until the baby asked for it. "The baby" or "baby girl" was all she'd called her throughout the pregnancy. She knew if Ross and Linda told her the name that they'd chosen then she would get attached. If she got attached, then she would've probably ruined everyone's life by trying to keep her daughter and raise her. But she was a seventeen-year-old girl without a friend in the world. She might have decided to lose her virginity too early in life, and she might have chosen the wrong guy to lose it to, but she wasn't dumb. She knew trying to raise her baby with no help would be disastrous.

The baby started to fuss, so she rocked her a little. "Chin up, baby girl. Your mom and dad are great, and you're going to have an amazing life. I love you more than my own soul, and that is why I am giving you your best chance. I know you'll make me proud. No matter who you are or who you grow to be. I'll love you forever even if you choose to never meet me."

The tears were streaming down her face in full force. There was no stopping them, but she was alone, so there was no one to care or judge. She'd given Ross and Linda the first hour after the birth and then asked if she could be alone with the baby for the second hour. She needed that time to say her proper goodbyes.

She laid there with the baby in her arms, her eyes closed, tears still in her eyes, and humming some hymn she'd grown up singing in church. She couldn't even remember the name of it or all the words, but the sweet melody felt right for the moment.

Before she knew it, the hour was up, and Linda was knocking on her door, followed closely by Ross. They both looked apologetic that they were intruding, so she smiled to let them know she was okay. She really was. Though her heart was breaking, she still knew she'd made the best decision.

As she handed the baby to Linda, she shifted in the bed and cringed when she remembered just how sore she still was. Giving birth was no joke, and she was not so sure she ever wanted to do it again.

"Are you all right? Can I get you anything?" Linda

really was a sweetheart. At that point, they could've taken the baby, moved to a different room until the baby was released from the hospital and never seen her again. But they just weren't those kinds of people.

"I'm okay, thanks." She hoped Linda understood she meant more than physically okay. She was okay with everything that was happening, too. "They should be delivering dinner soon. And the nurse said she'd be back to help me change." And go to the bathroom, but she wasn't going to mention that with Ross in the room.

"We'll take the baby to the nursery for a bit to get out of your hair." Before she could respond, Linda jumped back in. "But don't worry. We will be right back after the nurse leaves. We want to give you your privacy, but you can't get rid of us that easily." She smiled so Stacey knew she was teasing, not crazy. It was an odd situation. No one quite knew where the line was, but she did know that she was grateful for the support, even if it came from an unlikely source. One of the reasons she'd chosen Ross and Linda was because they already understood a little about what she was going through.

Before they decided to adopt, they tried one round of IVF and it was successful. Linda had an easy, textbook pregnancy, but there were complications during the delivery. Despite all the interventions available, their baby was born sleeping. She never asked for more of the story than Linda was willing to offer, but it was enough to know that she already knew what it was like to enter a hospital pregnant and leave without a baby. Something Stacey would soon be experiencing. Not that she would wish that on anyone, and she wasn't specifically looking for that when she was deciding on adoptive parents. But it gave her the feeling that she and Linda were kindred spirits, and maybe the best people to raise her baby were the people her gut chose.

With the tub full and the bottle half empty, she turned off the water and smiled. Everything had turned out okay in the end. Her parents kicked her out when she was pregnant, and she lived in a group home for pregnant girls and mothers until she gave birth. Hello Bible study and chores, though it really wasn't much different than home. Since she elected for adoption, she wasn't technically a mother in their eyes, so they kicked her out far too soon after the baby was born.

She called her dad's sister, the other black sheep of the family, who helped her get emancipated and bought her a bus ticket from Houston to San Diego, and she never looked back.

Since her aunt and her father were estranged, she didn't really know her until she moved in with her, but in a short time, they grew closer than she ever felt to her parents.

Her Aunt Brenda never had kids. She'd chosen the single artist life over settling down "under a man's thumb and surrounded by ankle biters that ruled her life" in her words. She only had a one-bedroom apartment in Hillcrest, which she called the art mecca of San Diego. But they made it work with Stacey sleeping on the pull-out couch until they could both move into a two-bedroom in the same apartment complex. She was just grateful for a bed and a roof and someone who loved her enough to take care of her until she figured everything out.

Thanks to her aunt, it didn't take long for her to find her bearings. At least, attending the accelerated school while she was pregnant meant she finished her classes right before she went into labor. She never walked with her classmates or attended prom, but after everything she'd experienced, that all seemed like small potatoes, anyway. She had other things to worry about, like finding a job and helping her aunt with rent. She said she was fine, and Stacey knew she was no starving artist, but she wanted to help, nonetheless. She'd been raised to help, always, in any way possible, and lifelong teachings like those didn't just go away.

Her first job was cashier at a grocery before she left to take an office job. At least the job at the office paid enough for her to find her own place, but it was stifling. She quickly figured out she wasn't cut out to work in a place so structured. She could do the work and had no problem working hard, but she liked to have fun and play hard too.

From there, she took a job managing a hair salon. She liked it for the most part, but a couple of the stylists treated her as nothing but their hair sweeper and errand girl. And the owner refused to do anything about it. She had to get out of there for her own sanity.

That was when she found the job at Kelly's. She'd never officially been a bartender. But living with an aunt who constantly entertained and taught her every drink in the book before she was even old enough to have a drink, was enough to impress the bar manager, Kelsey.

Bartending had been her favorite job until the job at the tattoo studio came along, so she was happy she could keep some hours there and not quit completely.

But, oh God, she had to go back there with her tail between her legs and apologize to Jesus. Just the thought deserved a large gulp from her bottle.

What was she supposed to say? *Hello. I'm sorry I misjudged you. I am thoroughly and irrevocably messed up in the head. Might as well get used to it because it will probably happen again.*

She'd spent the last seven years "moving on", but she hadn't really moved on if it was still affecting her. What she'd actually done was close herself off from having a deep, meaningful relationship with anyone, except Aunt Brenda, so that she just never had to deal with being caught vulnerable again.

So how had she reached that place with Jesus? When had he wormed his way in, so she cared what he thought of her? How had he done it? It wasn't the sex. That was hate-sex. It was just supposed to get him out of her system. Turns out that was easier said than done.

Her bath water turned cold, and she reached the bottom of her bottle before she could figure anything out.

Chapter Eleven

Jesus

An appointment with a regular client brought him back to the shop for the first time in days since Stacey sped away from him with no explanation. In all honesty, he was both excited and dreading his next encounter with her. The cold-shoulder-Stacey he'd known for so long was fun to antagonize, but he was just getting used to the sweet-Stacey that everyone else knew, and he liked her. And oh God, the sexy Stacey bent over his bench that only he knew sent the blood straight to his cock every time he allowed himself to think about it.

Something changed the other night. She'd caught him off-guard with her assumptions, but he still blamed himself for running her off. Ashamed he'd lost his temper, he knew he shouldn't have been so harsh, but he hadn't expected her to run either. She just left—leaving him with questions upon questions, and days to stew over them. Calling her seemed out of the question. He felt that whatever they had to say to each other needed to be in person.

She avoided him for the first few hours he was there. The client with an appointment came and went for his second session of a four-session sleeve. The tattoo would be epic when it was done. He managed to get in the zone and fully focus on his art while his client was there, but his mind started to wander once he left.

"Knock. Knock."

Normally, he'd roll his eyes at someone who spoke their knocks, but he knew that sweet voice and it wasn't like he was paying attention to his surroundings or actually had a door for her to knock on.

"*Hola, mariposa.*"

"Hey." He could tell she was nervous to say something. "I, uh… I wanted to apologize for taking off like that the other night. I just kind of panicked, I guess. I didn't mean to offend you. Apparently, I'm just socially awkward and kind of terrible at reading people. Can I buy you a drink later to make up for it?"

"You don't have to do that."

"I want to. I think it's the least I can do."

He nodded his head. He didn't want her to feel like she owed him anything, but he did want the opportunity to talk to her. "Okay. Sure. Let's do it. I'm packing up to leave now. When are you off?"

"I get off at eight."

"So, Kelly's at nine?"

"Can we go somewhere else?"

He wondered why but didn't ask. "Of course, *mariposa*. Anywhere you like."

Sitting all alone at a tiny table in a bar he'd never been to a few hours later was the most uncomfortable he'd felt in a long time. He arrived early on purpose to beat her there, but she was running so late he was beginning to fear she'd stood him up.

Shaking her hips like a novice runway model the flirty waitress, Candice, came by again to ask if he needed anything. He remained polite and declined while every cell in his body screamed, "Fuck off!" The woman should've just tattooed "Trying too hard" on her forehead and saved everyone some time. Only halfway through his second beer, clearly, he was nursing his alcohol, so he didn't drink too much before Stacey got there. Any good waitress would be able to read that and back off.

He took a deep breath, realizing he was agitated and being overly harsh. Growing up with four older sisters taught him to recognize emotions in others, but like most people, he was sometimes slow to recognize his own. The problem wasn't the waitress. Well, not *all* the waitress. It was him. Frustrated that Stacey was over half an hour late, he needed to accept that she'd stood him up and go home before he blew up at another woman who didn't deserve it.

He figured he might as well get home at a decent hour, so he had the time and energy to work out before he opened the studio the next day.

But before he could stand up, he spotted someone moving towards his table and his heart leaped so high in his chest, he nearly choked on it.

"Hey there. Did you think I wasn't coming?"

The thoughts in his head warred between being polite, making a "coming" joke, and sarcasm. "You're here now. That's all that matters." Politeness won, but at least it was also the truth. He took her smile to mean it was also the correct response in her eyes. Bonus points for him!

Complete with a frown on her face at Stacey's arrival, the waitress stomped up to the table, took her drink order, and barely gave him a second to ask for another beer before leaving again in a huff.

Her attitude didn't go unnoticed by Stacey. "Who put the bee in her bonnet?"

"I did, I guess. I think she thought I was lying when I said I was here to meet someone, or she hoped you wouldn't show up." He shrugged his shoulders. It wasn't his fault she didn't believe him.

"Well, I almost didn't."

"What?"

"I almost chickened out, and then I got here and almost chickened out again."

"Why?"

"I don't know." It was her turn to shrug her shoulders. "I'm not great at admitting when I'm wrong or facing someone when I've made a fool of myself."

"You haven't made a fool of yourself."

She scoffed. "Of course, I did. I ignored you after we, umm, hooked up." She whispered that last part like anyone could hear them over the dull roar of the bar. Even he had to read her lips to understand what she said. "I accused you of basically being a terrible person, and then I ran when I found out I was wrong."

"That's nothing. Call me when you break your ankle jumping off a balcony for no other reason than to impress a girl. Spoiler alert: She was not impressed."

He assumed the belly laughs meant she wasn't thinking of her own embarrassment anymore. "You really did that?" She was still laughing as Candice pounded their drinks on the table. That waitress was damn near on his last nerve. Maybe he could convince Stacey to bar hop to the place he saw just down the road. It was more crowded, but that would mean they'd be bothered less.

"I did. In my younger days. I'd just gotten out of the Marines. Thought I had something to prove to my buddies back home." He shrugged. "Thankfully, I grew up after that. Realized I had nothing to prove to them, or the girls in my hometown for that matter. As soon as I was healed, I hightailed it back to San Diego. Caught the first plane out of Texas, and now, visits are enough for me."

She huffed. "I won't even go back for those."

"Where? Home?"

"Yeah. Home. Texas."

"You're from Texas, too? Small world. What part?"

"Houston. You?"

"Same. Well, just outside in suburbia."

She cracked a smile. "Me too. Which side?"

"South, and let me guess, you're from the North side."

"No." She smirked. "West."

He groaned. "Oh, even worse." They both laughed. "So, what brought you out here?"

Her smile fell into a frown in an instant. "I, uh, moved in with my aunt."

"Oh yeah? Just picked up and moved cross-country for the hell of it?"

"Sure did. So, you're a Texas boy. I never would have guessed."

Wow. Smooth subject change. She wouldn't appreciate his sarcasm if he said that out loud, so he rolled with it without calling her out. "I get that a lot. More and more the longer I'm out here on the west coast. I do feel more at home out here."

"How long have you lived in San Diego?"

"Well, I got out about eight years ago and spent almost a year back home trying to make that work before I realized I belonged here. So, seven years. You?"

"About the same, actually. How long were you in?"

He saw where she was going and decided to just answer the question she was leading up to. "My enlistment was five years long, and I joined when

I was eighteen. That means I turn the big 3-1 this year."

Her eyebrows hit her hairline in surprise. Either she hadn't expected him to connect the dots, or he was older than she thought he was.

She schooled her features and recovered quickly, though. "I would not have guessed. Are you doing anything special for your birthday?"

"Don't know yet. It's not for a few months. I rarely think that far ahead unless I have to. So, what about you?"

"What about me what?"

He was hoping she'd think he was blatantly asking her age and blurt it out, but no such luck. "What did you do before moving out here?"

"Oh. I thought you were asking what I was going to do for my birthday this year. I don't know yet."

Assuming she would keep talking and answer his question, he waited, but she didn't offer anything more. "Nuh uh. Quit changing the subject when I ask you a question. I understand if you don't want to talk about everything, but give me something." He'd used his best dramatic soap opera voice to make her laugh, and it worked. Sort of. He got a smirk out of her.

"I graduated high school just before I moved out here. But before you go trying to do math in that pretty head of yours, I graduated early at seventeen, so I'm only twenty-four."

He didn't know whether to feel complimented, shocked, offended, or all three. He was actually good at math. But she'd also called him "pretty", and a primal part of him loved that she found him attractive. She was really twenty-four? He did his best to keep his face blank while he processed the information. Clearly, they'd both estimated each other's ages wrong in opposite directions, but he'd take his cue from her and not dwell on their age difference. It wasn't that big, after all.

"Are you some kind of genius?"

"No. I never struggled much in school, but just about anyone can graduate early if they are motivated enough."

There was a sadness to her voice that broke his heart, but he got the feeling she wouldn't elaborate if he asked, so he was the one to change the subject all together that time. "So. How are you liking the tattoo studio?"

She gave him what looked like a grateful smile. "I am enjoying myself. It's the challenge I don't have at the bar, but with the same fun, laid-back atmosphere. I can see myself sticking around for a while. How long have you been there?"

"A few years. I apprenticed at another shop and then worked there for years before Jeff hired me. Well, poached me, really. We were both artists at that shop before he came into some money, decided to open his own, and offered me a position." The idea of starting Day-One with a shop instead of trying to fit in to an established shop had sounded very appealing. Even after years at that shop, he'd still felt like "the new guy". An outsider. "What about Kelly's? Are you going to quit?"

"No. Not for now anyway. I do still like it there. I just won't have to fight to get an adequate number of hours on the schedule anymore. Kelsey, the manager, schedules based on seniority, and you'd have to burn down the place to get fired. So that leaves a few pretty inept bartenders working most of the prime tipping hours. It's maddening that even after a year, a quality job doesn't mean as much as time with the company. Not that they're all bad, or that I'm the best, or anything. I'm really just bitching about one or two. Don't mind me. I'm not usually this critical of my coworkers."

"I know exactly what you mean." He smiled at her, and she smiled back. He was finally really getting to know the sweet Stacey that everyone else got to meet eons ago. He didn't know why she'd chosen to paint him with such a broad brush, but he did regret that it had taken so long to get to know her. She was just very genuine, and it turned out they had a lot in common so far. The more he knew about her, the more he wanted to know about her. That didn't always happen for him. He got bored easily. He wanted to brush it off as a side-effect of being lonely, but it felt like more than that, if he was honest with himself.

"What?"

"What? What?"

"You're grinning at me. Why? Do I have something in my teeth?"

"No. Just glad we're finally doing this. I've been wanting to get to know you for a while, but you wouldn't give me the time of day."

"I'm really sorry about that." She looked sheepish. He didn't want that.

"No. I get it. Especially considering what you thought of me. I'm just glad we got everything cleared up."

They sat there for a minute smiling at each other like a couple of goobers, but it wasn't the awkward moment it should have been or used to be. Now that everything was out in the open, sitting with her in silence felt as easy as breathing.

A waitress he'd never seen before sidled up to the table. "Hey, my name's Annie. Candice didn't feel well and went home early, so I'll be your server now. Are either of you ready for another beer?"

Happy to hear they wouldn't have to change venues because of their waitress, he picked up his beer that he'd only taken a couple of sips of. "I'm good. What about you, Stacey?"

Hers was almost full, too. "I'm great." She looked at him when she said that though, and he felt like she meant more than the status of her drink. He grinned at her, and his heart flip-flopped when she smiled back.

Small talking until their beers were empty, he was hesitant to drink the last of it and burst whatever magic bubble they were in, but he could see the fatigue clear on her face and he imagined he looked much the same.

As if she could read his mind, she checked the time on her phone. "I didn't realize it was so late. I need to get home."

She flagged down their new waitress and paid for their beers. He wanted to protest but knew she would just fight him about it and say she owed him. At least he'd already paid cash for the first two he had before she got there. As they headed for the door, he resisted the urge to grab her hand. Instead, he stuck one hand in his pocket and placed the other on the small of her back. It was innocent enough. Just something men did to guide a girl through the crowd and let her know that he was right behind her. But the little bit of contact only made him want more.

Like the gentleman he was, he spotted her car and walked her to it. He didn't make the same mistake of standing on the other side of her door, though.

Before he opened her door for her, he had to know something. "Can I see you again?"

"I'll see you at work tomorrow. Won't I?"

"Yeah, but can I take you out again?"

"Sure. I'd love to go for drinks again. Maybe we can invite some of the other guys from the studio next time."

He growled. It wasn't going at all how he'd planned. "No. Just us. A date. I want to take you on a date."

She was chuckling.

Fuck me. She's messing with me.

But her giggles were infectious. He started chuckling too.

"I'm sorry, Jesus. I know I'm sending mixed signals, but the other night wasn't supposed to be the start of something. I don't date guys I work with."

He understood. It was a good rule. It was usually his rule. Of course, not sleeping with his coworkers was also a rule. Come to think of it, not sleeping with coworkers at work was definitely a rule he should've considered having, but he'd never been in the situation to need it before. Good thing he already knew that she was worth breaking all the rules for.

He took a chance and moved a little closer to her. If she'd backed up, he would too, but she didn't. That spoke volumes to him. It told him he had a chance, even if it was a miniscule one.

"I get it. I do. I live by the same rule, and I've never seriously wanted to break it until you. Tonight was amazing for so many reasons, and yet all we did was have a drink at a bar. Just the thought of filling my life with nights like tonight is worth all the risks. Don't you feel it? If you don't, just tell me, and I'll never bring it up again."

Though it would be the hardest thing he'd ever done.

Chapter Twelve

Stacey

Do I feel it?

As close as they were standing, she felt like she was audibly buzzing. Practically on fire with anticipation, she agreed there was potentially something special between them. She hadn't felt half as excited about a guy since... *Nope. He doesn't get this moment.*

She looked into Jesus's eyes as he moved her hair behind her ear, traced the line of her jaw and held her chin so feather light and tender. Not really holding her in place, but like a super magnet, she couldn't have moved if she'd wanted to. Emphasis on the "if".

Oh my God. He's going to kiss me.

Holding eye contact, he came closer and closer, so slowly she almost bit his head off and told him to kiss her already.

When she couldn't take it anymore, she took matters into her own hands and rushed up to meet his kiss. Logically, she knew it was the wrong move, but her hormones weren't listening, and they were running the show at the moment.

He smiled against her lips before his hand moved from her chin to the back of her neck under her hair. The other wrapped around her waist, plastering her upper body to him. Her hands traveled from his waist to his back, up to his shoulders and back down, exploring the body she didn't get a chance to properly feel the other night.

He was solid all over. The hard plains of his chest and abs against the soft curves of her body as his lips explored hers were enough to short circuit her brain. He licked her lips to ask for entrance and she opened for him, meeting his tongue with her own as they got lost in each other. The back and forth was like a dance that didn't need music. He was taller than her, but not by much and the way their bodies fit together felt perfect in every way. He tasted like beer, smelled like soap, and felt like sin. She was damned for sure.

Her aunt always told her that the way a man kissed was a prelude to the way they fucked, and she'd been with enough men to test that theory. They may have done things backwards when they fucked before any kissing, but considering how well he did both, Jesus was definitely ahead of the curve. The thought made her giggle.

"Is that a 'yes'?"

"Hmm?" She was still in a daze and only mildly aware that they'd stopped kissing.

He chuckled. "Can I take you out again? Will you

take a chance on me? On us?"

Would she? Could she?

Her silence must've been answer enough.

"I'll let you think it over. I'll admit I'm having a little trouble thinking straight after that kiss, too." He winked at her, and she laughed. "But I will not give up. You just feel too important to give up on without a fight."

She was right all along. He was a smooth talker, but it turned out that his smooth words felt authentic, too. She remembered the last time she'd felt swept off her feet. She was a naïve kid then, but she wasn't one anymore. She couldn't let smooth words, authentic or not, and an amazing kiss, cloud her judgment.

If she was being honest with herself, once she got past her own misconceptions about him, and allowed herself to see the real Jesus, she could see how he might become special to her. But was she where he was? She didn't think so. At least, not yet.

"I'll think about it." Her words said one thing, but inside, her walls were already crumbling beneath his charm and the undeniable connection becoming clear between them.

He grinned and kissed her again. It wasn't a peck, but it was downright chaste compared to their first kiss. She was almost disappointed. Maybe that was her answer, but also maybe that was her hormones talking still. The fact that she wasn't sure was what scared her the most and why she needed to think without the delectable man on her mind staring at her. She did not have it in her to misjudge another man.

"Call me or at least text me when you get home, so I know you made it safe."

Well, that made her all warm and fuzzy inside. "Okay. I will."

He opened her door for her and closed it again once she was seated.

She rolled down her window. "And you, too. Let me know. You know, you made it."

Smooth.

She wanted to bang her head on her steering wheel. There was no way he understood what she was saying through the broken gibberish.

Trying—and failing—to hold back his laughter, he responded, "*Gracias, mariposa.* I will."

As much as she could without causing an accident, she watched him watch her as she drove away. Any other man would've creeped her out doing that, but Jesus made her feel... What was the word? Safe? Protected? Wanted? Loved? That was crazy, but it was easy to see the potential there. Maybe she didn't need as much time as she thought. Who knew just driving away from him, again, would kick her decisions into high gear?

Though she was far enough away not to be able to see him anymore, she imagined him still standing in the same spot as though he had long-range x-ray vision, and that only made her giddier. Damn, she was weird.

Suffice to say, the night had far exceeded

her expectations. She'd imagined long awkward silences, and lots of alcohol to set the extrovert side of her free. But instead of a warm belly full of beer, she'd left with a warm, full heart for the first time in a long time. That was something to sit up and take notice of, but was it enough to build something on? That was the point of dating. Right?

∞∞∞

Jesus

As he was getting in his Chevelle to leave the bar, his cell phone rang in his pocket. Seeing one of his sisters calling him when it was after midnight in Texas instantly worried him. Given that it was his youngest older sister, Natalia, calling him though meant that it could be anything from boredom to an actual emergency.

"What's going on, Nat?"

"Hey bro! Not much. What's up with you?"

He breathed a sigh of relief that there didn't seem to be a family emergency brewing. "Driving home. Why are you calling so late?"

"Ugh. Leo is working late, and I won't be able to sleep until I know he's home safe. With the time difference, I knew you'd still be up. Keep me company for a little while?"

"Yeah, sis. Of course." His sister's husband was

a paramedic, and he knew she worried about him when he worked late. Jesus put in his earbuds and set his phone aside, so he had his hands free to shift as he got on the road towards home. He loved his classic car, but sometimes it'd be nice to have built-in Bluetooth.

"So, why are you just going home? Late night at the studio?"

He knew the question was coming, but he still hadn't decided what to say. "No. Leaving the bar."

"Oh? Drinks with the guys? Tell them I said hi."

"Uh, no…"

"No? Was it a date?"

"Not quite. I don't know. It's complicated."

"The best stories usually are. Tell me about her."

"Nat." He sighed. "Maybe you can help me out, but you can't tell the others. I don't need a phone call from *Mami* begging for more *nietos* again."

She just cackled at him. He should've known he'd get no sympathy from her. "Oh, come on, Jesus. You know she could have a hundred grandkids and still want more. Especially from her baby boy. That's never going to change. But I won't tell. You know that."

He did know. Of all his sisters, he was closest to Natalia, and he could always trust her with his secrets and true feelings. "Yeah, Nat. I know. I'm just feeling differently about this girl, and I don't need a bunch of other opinions floating around my head before I've formed my own thoughts."

"Wow, Jesus. I don't think I've ever heard you

talk about a girl like this."

"There are no other girls like this."

Silence. Jesus glanced at his phone to make sure the call was still connected. It was.

"Nat?"

"Sorry, baby bro. Didn't mean to disappear on you there, but that was beautiful. I can't wait to meet her."

"Oh? Planning a trip to California in the near future?"

"I don't know. Is that what it's going to take to see you?"

"Touché, sis." How often he visited Texas had become a point of contention between him and his family. He knew it was easier for him to travel to them than the other way around, but when it was time to go home, no matter how long he'd stayed, it wasn't long enough. Somehow, he managed to disappoint them because anything less than forever was too short. Like his parents were just waiting for him to give up the silly notion that California was his home now.

"I'm sorry, *hermano*. I know that's a sore subject."

"Don't worry about it, Nat. It is what it is. Plus, if we're talking about bringing her home with me, we're not quite there yet anyway."

"'Not quite there'? Like you're going to be there, eventually? Aww, Jesus. Seriously, I'm a puddle of goo over here. What's she like?"

"She's…" He took a moment to think about it.

"She's warm and sweet and smart and fuckin' beautiful. Like damn, you know? But she just started as the manager at the studio, and I haven't had an actual relationship in ages. What if I suck at it? What if I screw it up and then we can't stand to be in the same room together? We've been there, done that, and I don't think I could go back to that. But it wouldn't be me leaving the studio. No. She'd feel like she's the one that has to leave, and then I'd be responsible for her giving up a job she really likes. I don't want to be that guy."

"Whoa. So many questions. What do you mean by 'been there, done that'? And don't be so pessimistic. You don't have to have everything figured out in the beginning. That's half the fun of a new relationship."

"She used to hate me." His sister started to interrupt, but he kept talking. "It was all over a misunderstanding, but you know me. I've basically spent months pushing her buttons because it made her get all cute and hot-headed. Now that we've cleared the air, though, I don't know what happens next. I asked her to take a chance on us, but was that crazy? I felt so sure of things when she was in my arms, but what if this just fucks everything up for her? I am so out of my depth here, Nat."

"First of all, you're right. This is uncharted territory for you, but that is not a bad thing. Second, I understand there is an added layer of risk in this situation, but every new relationship is a gamble. You can go for it and let the chips land where they may, or you can play it safe. You can choose to never put yourself out there, but the way you've talked about this girl makes me think that you'd always wonder what could've been. Do you really want to take the chance of having to sit back and watch her date other people just because y'all decided to play it safe?"

"Fuck no."

"And third, do you trust that she is a big girl, and if she does decide to be with you that she has thought through the consequences and made her decision with her eyes wide open?"

"Yes. Of course."

"Then what's the problem?"

"Uhhh."

"That's what I thought."

"The problem is, I thought I was talking to the cool big sister, not the bossy one."

"Eh, we're all bossy when we need to be. It's our big sister right to boss around the baby brother."

"I hate you."

"Nah, you love me, and I love you. And Leo just walked in the door, so I have to go. Talk later?"

"Yeah, Nat. Talk later."

They hung up, and he drove the rest of the way home in silence. Momentary freakouts aside, he was surer than ever that he wanted to spend a lot more time with Stacey.

Chapter Thirteen

Stacey

Jesus sat down on his usual stool at the bar. "Can I get a Miller Lite?"

Expecting him to say "Guinness", her hand was already reaching for a tulip glass. "No Guinness?"

"Nah. I want something light. I'm saving my liver for Will and Nikki's wedding tomorrow."

"Wedding? That's tomorrow?"

"Yeah. They're having a quick, small ceremony in their backyard with friends and family. They both said they're practically married, and the ceremony is just a formality and a reason to have a party."

"Wow. Well, good for all of them. Tell them I said 'congratulations'." She rolled her eyes at herself. "If they even remember who I am."

"Of course, they know who you are. They wouldn't forget their favorite bartender at their favorite bar."

That was a stretch.

122

"In fact, why don't you come? You can be my 'plus one'. Do you work tomorrow? It starts at six."

"Umm…" She didn't know how to answer that. Especially since he was inviting her to a wedding. Didn't you have to RSVP to those things in advance? On the one hand, she wanted to go to wish them well herself, but she was not keen to go as his date. She didn't know what they were, but "dating" wasn't it. They might've cleared the air and admitted their attraction to one another, but she was serious when she said she didn't date coworkers.

As if conjured by their conversation, the man and woman they were discussing came in and she was spared from answering him anyway.

"Jesus. Should've known I'd see you here, but I would've assumed later. Not working tonight?" Will sat next to Jesus as he asked him the question, and Nikki sat next to Will.

"I opened, so I just got off."

"What? Out of bed before noon?"

"Hey." He laughed. "I will meet my clients any time they want. I'd always rather have a client that takes the time to make an appointment and sit with me for a minute on a design concept than a walk-in with a half-baked idea after half a bottle of tequila. Plus, I had to stop by and bug Stacey. It's basically tradition at this point. I can't monopolize her time at the studio without hearing about it from Jeff."

"The studio? You're not leaving Kelly's, are you?"

Nikki's question took her a little off guard. Not the nature of her question, but the concern in her voice, like she actually cared whether she left Kelly's.

"No. I'll still work here, but the hours aren't stable enough, and it just so happens that Jesus's shop needed a manager."

"It's not my shop."

"It could be."

That tidbit from Will was unexpected. What does he mean?

"Shut up, man. I don't know if I'm interested."

She looked quizzically back and forth between the men, but neither continued. Not that it was any of her business. She'd just gotten used to people telling her things just because she was there serving them a drink.

Speaking of... "Will. Nikki. What can I get you?"

They ordered their usual, a Long Island Iced Tea for her and a beer for him. And then she left them to talk while she took care of some other customers.

When she returned, all three of them were laughing for whatever reason, and it hit her that she had not had a group of friends to laugh with in a long time.

"What are you doing tomorrow, Stacey?" Nikki asked.

"Oh, I don't know. It's my first Saturday off in a while."

"I thought you were coming to the wedding

with me."

"No. I never said that."

"Well, I would love it if you could make it to our wedding. Sorry for the short notice, but I don't have your number. Actually, let's remedy that now." Nikki handed Stacey her phone. "Put your number in my phone." She paused and got a panicked look on her face. "Umm… if that's okay. I mean. That came out a little pushy. Will says I'm bossy, but I tell him it's because I work with eight-year-olds. Then he says that he's not an eight-year-old, but I still boss him around. And I say that if he wants me to stop bossing him around, then he needs to stop acting like an eight-year-old. And… I'm blabbering. Can I get your number, Stacey? I'd love to hang out sometime if you're interested."

Stacey could not figure out what was happening. Had Jesus put Nikki up to it? But why would he? Was she really interested in hanging out? A friend who wasn't her aunt's age would be nice. She added her number and handed Nikki back her phone.

"Great. I'll text you the details. I'd really love it if you could come."

"Okay. I'll think about it and let you know."

"Oh, okay. Yeah, that's good."

"So, are you registered anywhere?" Just in case she did decide to go.

"Oh, no. No presents. Just bring yourself. We don't need anything."

She understood what Nikki was saying. They'd

apparently already been living together, and they'd both been married before. But if there was one thing her mom taught her that she still agreed with, it was that you didn't show up to a wedding empty handed.

The next day, Stacey arrived at Will and Nikki's home right on time, but she still had to park way down the street. Wishing she'd picked a smaller gift, she walked down the sidewalk, praying she didn't trip on anything. She did not have a free hand to catch herself if she fell.

There were signs directing guests into the backyard via the gate instead of going through the house. She quickly found the presents table and set her gift down. She wasn't the only one who ignored the "no gifts" rule. Then she looked around the beautifully decorated space for a place to sit.

Of course, Jesus was already seated and waving her down from the second row like a lunatic. She battled with herself about whether it would cause a bigger scene to wave him off and sit in the back, or to walk all the way to the front and sit with him. Imagining him throwing her over his shoulder and carrying her to the seat next to him in front of everyone, both embarrassed her and turned her on.

As confusing as that was, she opted to calmly walk up to the second row and take the seat offered, even if she didn't feel she deserved to sit with the family and close friends of the bride and groom. She was just their bartender.

"I'm glad you could make it, *mariposa*. You look beautiful."

"Thank you." She was pretty proud of her outfit. Her floral sundress and strappy sandals were completely outside her comfort zone but fit in well for the wedding. "You look nice, too. I kind of expected you to be dressed like a groomsman and standing next to the altar."

"Oh, well, Will said if he chose one of his brothers, he'd have to choose all of us to stand with him, and Nikki refused to ask half the teaching staff at her school just to fill all the bridesmaid's spots. They decided on a best man and maid of honor, and that's it."

When the ceremony started, Stacey saw the best man was Will's son, Joe, and the maid of honor was Nikki's best friend, Joyce. She had to agree that those choices were perfect and much better than a twenty-person wedding party.

The ceremony was so beautiful that it brought tears to her eyes, and she wasn't alone. Everyone stood and cheered when the officiant pronounced them husband and wife.

"I told you no gifts!" Nikki found her once the reception started.

"I couldn't come empty-handed. It's really just for fun, anyway. How did you even notice my gift on the table with the others?"

"It's a basket of liquor bottles. You think we didn't zero in on it the moment we walked by the table?"

"Will! Bring the basket over here!"

"Coming, dear." Will's voice was laced with sarcasm, and Nikki swatted his arm when he reached them, making Stacey laugh. She loved how cute they were together.

Will set the basket on the table next to where they were standing. "What do we have here?"

Nikki started digging through the basket. "It's everything that goes into a Long Island Iced Tea and a book called <u>The Best Long Island Iced Tea Even a Doofus Could Make</u>. Whoa. That title is almost longer than the book itself. And it has pictures! That's perfect for you, Will."

Everybody laughed, and it was Will's turn to do the swatting, only he picked her ass.

Stacey was glad her gift was such a hit. She gave the bride and groom a hug as they left with their gift to mingle.

"Hey, Stace. Great gift!"

She turned to see Jesus right behind her. "Don't call me that."

The sternness in her voice got the message across because Jesus's eyebrows shot up. "Noted."

She almost felt bad for him. She didn't mean to come off as so bitchy, but she really hated that name. "And umm... thanks."

That made him smile, which was always contagious. Damn him.

"But really, good idea. I couldn't think of anything that clever, so I got them a gift card to the putt-putt place where they had their second date. I figured it was a good memory of their relationship and Will is always looking for activities to do with Joe. Plus, *mi mamá* always said not to show up to a wedding empty handed."

"Oh yeah? Did you grow up wealthy too?"

She knew the moment she said it that she couldn't undo her mistake. She never mentioned that to people, but it was exactly what she'd heard growing up.

"No. Mexican." He chuckled at that. "*Mi mamá* had a million rules for what you should and shouldn't do. Did you say 'wealthy'?"

"Umm… no… What?"

She tried to walk away, but he stopped her.

"Just drop it. Okay? I didn't mean to say what I said, and I don't want to talk about it."

He nodded his head once. "Okay. Can I get you a drink?"

She smiled. Hallelujah. A man who listens. "Sure. Why not? I've served you hundreds, maybe thousands, of drinks. Let's even up the score."

He chuckled at her sarcasm as they walked over to the bar. Though "bar" was a loose term. More like a table loaded with liquor and mixers so people could make whatever their heart desired.

"What's your poison?"

She thought for a moment. For once, she could order anything. She didn't have to work that night and she wasn't leaving the reception for hours, so she could go a little heavy on the alcohol for her first drink. "Do you see any Campari on the table?"

"Campari?"

"Yeah. It's a bitters."

"I know what it is." He searched the table for a second before picking up a clear bottle filled with a red liquid.

"So, what am I making?"

"Ever heard of a Negroni?"

"I have. It's made with gin. Right?"

"Yep. And Vermouth Rosso. I think I saw that over..." She looked over the bottles, selected the right one, and handed it to him. "Here."

"Thanks."

In equal parts, he added the three ingredients to a glass of ice. Then he winked at her and added a little more gin. She laughed at his antics as he stirred the drink and handed it to her.

She tasted the cocktail. Color her impressed. "So where did you learn to make Negroni's? And how did you know I like a little extra gin?"

"Just a hunch." He smiled at her. "I had a short-lived career as a bartender when I was apprenticing. Very short-lived. Just long enough to find out it wasn't for me."

"Well, thank you. It's my favorite, so I'm just glad you knew what it was."

"Your favorite, huh? I'll have to remember that." She ignored his flirty comment and kept her attention on the drink in her hand.

He began making another, and the look on her face must have shown her confusion.

"What? It sounded good." He laughed, and she smiled.

He tasted the drink he made. "Hey. That's pretty good. Maybe I should ask you to pick out all my drinks from now on."

"So now I have to pour all your beers and pick all your drinks?"

He had the good sense to look a little sheepish. "You remember that, huh?"

"How could I forget a conversation about your—how did you put it—your needs?"

Throwing his head and laughing, he caught the attention of nearly everyone around them but didn't seem to care.

"Yes, indeed. How could you forget?" He winked at her, and she blushed.

Damn him.

Chapter Fourteen

Jesus

He loved that blush on her and he loved being the reason for it, but recognized she didn't appreciate the attention they were getting together.

"Well, I need to mingle. See ya later. Don't do anything I wouldn't do." He threw that last part in for comic relief, and she snorted, so he counted it as a success.

He walked away but spent the entire reception completely aware of where she was at all times. He paid attention to who she spoke to and whether she seemed to have a good time or not. Creepy? Maybe, but it was involuntary. He was drawn to her, but by either accident or her design, their paths never crossed again at the reception.

As it drew to a close, he looked around and realized he missed her exit. She'd slipped out during one of the few brief moments when he wasn't staring at her like a creeper. It was just as well. She wasn't his yet, and he could appreciate that meant they didn't need to hang around arm in arm.

He found Joe and offered video games and movies for the rest of the night. He'd cleared it with Joe's parents—all four of them—before the wedding. They all appreciated that he still welcomed Joe over for sleepovers from time to time, and he knew they would all be exhausted after the wedding.

The next day, they all slept in and had another lazy Sunday morning until they realized all the roommates were home at the same time for once. So, they threw together an impromptu belated bar-b-que to welcome their new roommate, BJ.

War and Jesus went on a beer and grocery run while the other two readied the grill, kitchen and backyard, with Joe to help them. When they got back, Adam took over seasoning the meat for the grill while Jesus made a potato salad, baked beans and rolls. Relegated to watching, BJ made himself useful by grabbing his Bluetooth speaker and starting some music.

With their bellies full and the sun setting, they lit the firepit and sat around it with beers in hand. They sent Joe home to his mom's house to get ready for school the next day, and the rest of them enjoyed the peace and contentedness of being well-fed and relaxed.

"This is great. Did y'all used to do this more often before I moved in?"

"I wouldn't say 'more often', but we've done it

a few times when our schedules lined up," Adam answered BJ's question. "We always intend to get together more, but life, you know?"

"Yeah."

The moment stretched out, but Jesus was never good with silence. "So, Beej, are you ever going to tell us what BJ stands for?"

He grinned at BJ, who scowled back at him. "No."

Adam chuckled. "Give it up, Jesus. He's obviously never going to tell you."

Jesus whipped his head to stare at Adam. "But he told you?"

"I didn't say that."

"So, you don't know?"

"I didn't say that either." Adam just grinned at Jesus like a cat that got the canary.

Not that he was surprised—Mr. Secrets knew everything—but damn, he really wanted to know, too. One day, he'd get it out of him. BJ, not Adam. Adam was a fucking vault when he knew something. He should've gone into the CIA after the Marines. In fact, Jesus wasn't fully convinced that he hadn't. Maybe the accountant gig was a cover.

"So, did you guys serve together? Or what?" He figured BJ would be curious about how they met and came to be roommates.

"You know how it is. Being Marines is almost like we're all from the same small town. War, Adam and I all crossed paths with each other at different times. Even figured out that at one time the three of us and Will were all in Afghanistan at the same time, but we didn't know it then. Well, War and I knew because we were with the same squadron, but we didn't know about the other two and they hadn't even met us at the time. We didn't become close friends, though, until we were all under the same roof."

They spent a few more hours around the fire pit sharing stories. Nothing was off limits. Bootcamp experiences, overbearing Gunnys, the girls they chased but ultimately lost, friends made and lost, and the world they saw on Uncle Sam's dime, just to name a few.

He got to know BJ much better and felt he could count him a friend after that night, but he also got to know the other two a little better too. Sometimes it was easy to lose himself in the life he'd created in the tattoo world, but nights like that reminded him not to discount the importance of keeping the friends who understood the Marine Corps chapter of his life too.

Chapter Fifteen

Stacey

"**W**ould you fit me in for a tattoo tonight before we leave? Do you have time?" She was closing with Jesus that night, so she figured it was the perfect time to get one done without an audience. It'd taken her the last three days to build up the courage to ask, but the shocked look on his face was almost enough to make her take the request back.

"You want a tattoo? From me?"

"Yeah." Though, now she was less sure. "Why? Is it a *faux pas* for me to ask?"

He shook his head and wiped the stunned look off his face. "No. Not all. I'm just surprised you'd ask me. What did you have in mind?"

She slid a piece of paper over to him of what she'd drawn. She wasn't an artist by any stretch, but she couldn't imagine trying to describe it either.

"Seventy times seven?"

She nodded. "It's from the Bible."

"I know. The book of Matthew. Peter asks Jesus how many times he should forgive his brother when he betrays him. Seven times? Jesus says no, seventy times seven."

It was her turn to be shocked.

"What? My name is Jesus. I come from a large Latino family in Texas. You think I didn't grow up in church?" He chuckled at her.

"I could've guessed that. Maybe. But growing up in church doesn't always mean remembering scripture. It usually means you played games on the back pew."

He threw his head back and laughed. "True. But in my case, it means my father is a pastor, and therefore I can quote a lot of scripture at you."

"Wow. That's—not what I was expecting. And you're still close with them?"

He gave her a funny look. "Of course, I am. They don't always understand me, and they wish I'd made some different choices in life, but we still get along all right." He shrugged like it was no big deal, but it was a huge deal to her. If she'd asked him to explain why his parents were so accepting and hers weren't, he probably couldn't, but she wasn't sure she would've understood it anyway.

"That's good. So, what do you think? Can you fit me in tonight?"

"Of course, *mariposa*. Whatever you want. I can't say no to you."

She smiled at him and left his station as the bell over the front door sounded.

A beautiful woman walked in who said she had an appointment with Jesus, and a part of her wanted to tell her he wasn't there. *Damn hormones.* He wasn't hers, and even if he was, he was capable of doing his job and remaining professional, no matter how beautiful the girl was. Her brain knew that, but Lord, tell her emotions that. She couldn't believe how crazy territorial she was feeling.

The day passed without lying to any clients and sending them home. She cleaned the shop while Jesus wrapped up his last scheduled tattoo.

He ushered the man out the front door, locked it behind him, and turned off the lights in the front of the store so no one would think they were still open.

"You ready?"

"As I'll ever be."

He smiled reassuringly at her. "Don't worry, *mariposa.* You're in good hands."

She shivered, remembering the last time he had his hand on her. *This is going to be torture. What was I thinking?*

Smirking at her like he knew exactly where her mind had gone, he walked with her back into his station area and had her sit in a chair that looked like it came from a dental office. Of course, he knew the images floating through her brain. His mind was always in the gutter. She just joined him there on occasion.

With his back to her, he put on a pair of black gloves and started setting up what he needed at the counter. "Where do you want this?"

"Oh, umm. I'm not positive. I was going to get your advice on that, but I was thinking over here." She put her right hand on her chest up by her left shoulder and looked up at him in question.

"That's a good place. I just would've suggested you wore a different shirt." She didn't like the shit-eating grin on his face. "In that t-shirt, there's not an easy way to get to that spot. You could've just moved over a tank top or unbuttoned a button-up shirt a little. A y-shirt, though, just has to come off." His grin got bigger.

She looked down at the offending shirt. "Damn it."

Whatever. She pulled the shirt off over her head. The man had been inside her. She was going to be shy now?

He walked over to her with a razor in his hand. Gently, he moved her bra strap off her shoulder and down her arm and shaved the faint downy hairs from her skin to prepare the tattoo area. Then he applied the stencil solution and pressed the stencil to her shoulder. He peeled it off and pointed to the full-length mirror hanging on the wall.

"Go check out the placement in the mirror."

She got up and went to the mirror. Once she looked past her breasts on display in a lacy bra that left nothing to the imagination, she saw the outline of her design on her shoulder and got excited. She imagined it as the piece of art it was going to be, and it was perfect.

He came up behind her and looked at her in the mirror. "Good? Last chance to change it."

"It's great." Turning back towards the chair, she rolled her eyes at herself. Why was she being so awkward?

"You can sit on the chair or lie back on the bench. I can work wherever you're comfortable."

She chose the chair. The bench held memories she was already having trouble putting out of her mind. While the stencil finished drying, they discussed colors as he poured a little of each color into tiny cups.

When the only thing left was to start the tattoo, he put one hand on her shoulder and raised his machine in the air. "Are you ready for this?"

"Yep. Hurt me good, Jesus."

Chuckling, he pressed the needle to her skin and drew the outline. When she'd chosen the placement, not only did she not consider the shirt she was wearing, but she also didn't think about the fact that his arms would rest on her chest and his face would be inches from hers.

Thinking—or trying not to think—about his lips on hers, she couldn't decide if they were more or less charged than they would've been if they hadn't already had sex. Either way, with her mind completely occupied on those images, the pain of the tattoo was taking a back seat. Not that she'd thank him for that or anything.

No. She would not thank him for the fact that

she could barely breathe because every breath was filled with his scent, or that the buzz of his machine was practically as effective as a vibrator on her clit.

"Do you need a break, *mariposa*?" Did he sound as breathless as she was or was that her imagination?

"No. I'm good."

"Are you sure? You're squirming. If you're uncomfortable, we can move."

"I'm not uncomfortable." Wrong. She was very uncomfortable, but not because of where she was sitting. She looked down to see the outline was done, and he was about to fill it in with color. Soon, the torture would be over.

He leaned back in and began in earnest, his urgency to finish the tattoo matching hers. Her breath came in pants like a bitch in heat. Her whole body reacted to his touch, and it had nothing to do with the needle in her skin.

"*Mariposa*, you're killing me here."

"I'm killing *you*?"

He chuckled, his breath ghosting across her oversensitive skin as he continued to work. "Yes. You're making it awfully hard to concentrate. It's a good thing I'm such an expert and can't be so easily distracted."

"Oh, yes. Lucky for me. How can I ever thank you?"

"I'm sure you'll think of something, *mariposa*."

She closed her eyes after that, leaned her head

back on the chair, and got lost in the sensations of the tattoo. If she wasn't looking at him, she could keep the effects he had on her to a minimum.

He was wiping down her completed tattoo and passing her a hand-held mirror before she realized the noise of the machine had stopped.

"What do you think, *mariposa*? Does it pass inspection?"

"It's beautiful. Thank you. Even better than I pictured."

"I'm glad you like it."

He rubbed the goo over the new tattoo, covered it with saran wrap, and used bandage tape to hold it in place. As he pressed the last edge down across the top of her shoulder, he skimmed his hand up her neck, cupped her jaw, and brought his lips to hers. A part of her rejoiced at finally getting what she needed, but it wasn't enough.

She brought her arms around him, pulling him closer to her, and moved her legs out of the way so he could get between them. Past caring about labels or expectations, she let her instincts take over.

"I need you, Jesus."

"I need you too, *mariposa*."

"So, take me."

He growled against her lips, and her core clenched. Grabbing the hem of his shirt, she pulled it over his head and finally got a glimpse of the abs she'd fantasized about.

"Jesus."

"Yeah baby, curse my name."

She smiled and swatted his arm. "Dork."

"Mmmm. That's right. Talk dirty to me."

She giggled, but the sound got caught in her throat and turned into a moan as he pulled the cups of her bra down and latched on to her nipple with his teeth. Unable to take it anymore, she started unbuttoning her own jeans, but Jesus took over for her and pulled them over her hips and down her legs, taking her underwear with them.

Before she could feel self-conscious sitting naked in his tattoo chair while he stood there almost fully dressed, he was dropping his pants, rolling a condom on—that seemingly came from nowhere—stepping back between her legs, and probing at her entrance.

"Next time, I promise to take my time with you, but I don't think I can wait this time. Are you ready for me, *mariposa*?"

"More than. Do it, Jesus. Fuck me."

He pulled her hips to the edge of the chair and kissed her as he slammed all the way home in a single thrust. They both moaned with their lips still pressed together.

She clawed his back and dug her heels into his ass, trying to meet his thrusts, but he held all the control as his fingers gripped her hips, holding her in place and taking her on the ride of her life.

"Jesus."

"Jesus."

"Jesus."

"Oh, God."

"Jesus."

"Yes, *mariposa*. Hang on. I'll get you there."

Letting go of one of her hips, he brought a hand to her core, tracing her lips where his cock passed in and out of her. Then, he brought his slick fingers to her clit, gliding around it before giving it all his attention, fluttering his fingers and sending her higher and higher.

Soon, the relentless pulsing cock and vibrations from his fingers sent her flying over the edge. She closed her eyes and saw fireworks behind her eyelids as she came, only barely aware that he was coming too. The warmth of his breath on her new tattoo where his head had become tucked in the crook of her neck made her feel satisfied and content in a way that she'd never felt before.

"Damn, *mariposa*. What you do to me."

She giggled, loving the feel of his softening cock still buried inside her. "I'm pretty sure we did it to each other."

His lips met hers and wouldn't let go. His tongue dipping in to taste her until only the need to breathe parted them.

"We did, *mariposa*. We did."

Grabbing the bottom of the condom, he pulled out of her and threw it away. Then, he gave her a spectacular view of his tattooed ass as he pulled up his jeans and boxers before he came back to her with her own jeans and underwear.

Then, he did the same with their shirts and

her bra, even helping her redress over the plastic covering her new tattoo. The sweetness of his actions drove home the feeling that she was so, so wrong about him before.

They worked together to sanitize and straighten his station before closing up the shop and walking out back to their cars.

"Are you okay to get home, *mariposa*? It's gotten late."

"Yes. I'll be fine. I don't live too far from here, but thank you for asking."

He kissed her long and sweet before opening her door for her and closing it when she was in safely. They left the parking lot together but drove off in opposite directions.

Chapter Sixteen

Jesus

"**G**reat job, Eric. Carry on." Inspecting his apprentice's line work before he moved on to the next phase was just a formality at that point. Eric knew what he was doing and was nearly ready to be left to his own devices. Soon, he would get his own chair and be responsible for bringing in his own clients. Jesus was happy for the kid—and the chair would be well deserved—but Eric was just a kid, and he still had a few things to work on. Namely, not rushing the final strokes of his machine.

Every tattoo by Eric was easy going until right at the end, when he would suddenly dash for the finish line. It was Jesus's goal to teach Eric to slow down before he declared him ready for his own chair. To Jesus, the last lines were the most crucial. A mistake in the beginning of a tattoo could be easily fixed, but a mistake at the end was a pain to fix and often glaringly obvious, even after being fixed.

He got up to stretch his legs and refresh his

coffee while Eric got started on the colors and shading. The client getting the tattoo was another of Jesus's long-time customers. Jesus trusted Eric to do a good job, and his client trusted Jesus. That was part of what he loved about being a tattooist.

He took the trust that others put in him to create permanent art on their bodies seriously, and his job was to pass that on to the next generation of tattoo artists. Especially in a time of instant gratification and where nothing was permanent, it was even more important for them to learn that tattoos were special. Even the smallest tattoos took time to create, and even with all the modern advancements in tattoo removal, tattoos were still stubbornly permanent.

"Are you going to drink that coffee or stare at it? Oh! Did it get cold? Are you heating it up with your laser vision?" Dillon dropped his voice to a conspiratorial whisper. "Are you really Superman? It's okay. I'll never tell anyone. Your secret's safe with me."

"*Gracias*, Dillon. I really appreciate that. You never know who you can trust with a secret that big, but I know I can count on you." His deadpan delivery almost cracked at the end, but Jesus held on.

They both laughed and then fist-bumped their hello's.

"Hey, Dillon. How was the trip?"

Dillon had taken a few weeks off to visit his family in Arizona. Something about a pregnant sister, his parents first grandbaby and a big party. With four sisters, Jesus could relate all too well.

"It was good. Saw everyone. Ran into some friends from high school. It was good. Fun."

Jesus chuckled. Dillon wasn't fooling anyone. "Good to visit, but great to come back?"

Dillon sighed. "Yeah. Does that make me a terrible person?"

"Nah. I get it. You outgrew your hometown. It's normal. Most of us do when we move away. Don't beat yourself up about it."

Dillon just shrugged.

"Hey, you want to come stand over Eric and make him nervous while he finishes this tattoo?"

"Fuck yeah."

Jesus chuckled as they walked back to the station that Eric shared with Jeff. Though with Jeff talking about stepping back, maybe it would just be Eric's station soon.

"Ten bucks says he rushes to finish the tattoo again." Dillon whispered to Jesus when they were far enough away that neither Eric nor the client would hear them.

"Fuck that. I'm not taking that bet. It'll be the easiest ten bucks you ever made."

"What? No confidence in your apprentice?"

"I have complete confidence in him. I just don't know if that particular lesson has completely sunk in yet."

Dillon snickered. "That was diplomatic."

"Well, you know me. Diplomatic as fuck."

For some reason, that was hilarious to Dillon, and he laughed loud enough to get the attention of both Eric and the client.

"Speaking of apprenticeships, where's Beau? Shouldn't you be learning the great art of piercing and body modification?"

"I think I've learned all I can in the pain game, but no, today I'm catching up on tattoo appointments. After a few weeks out, I had back-to-back tattoo clients lined up today, but one of them rescheduled at the last minute. I checked in with Beau, and he's clientless right now too, so I guess I'll take the next walk-in. Until then, I'm all yours, baby."

Dillon winked.

"Goody for me. What do you want to do first? Braid each other's hair? Tell ghost stories? Or share our biggest crushes?"

"Well, braiding our hair is probably out. I could braid yours if I knew what I was doing, but I don't have anything long enough for you to braid."

"I love the way you worded that. Like you knew I'd bring up your leg hair or sack hair if you left it open for me."

They both snickered.

"No braiding." Dillon shot Jesus a stern look, but then couldn't help but smile. "I don't think I know any ghost stories, so that leaves crushes. Who are you crushing on, Jesus?" Then he winked. The fucker.

"Oh, right for the jugular." Jesus chuckled. Why,

oh why, did he bring *that* up? He walked into his own joke. He was officially an idiot.

"Okay. Okay. I'll go first." Dillon paused for dramatic effect. "Hmm. No one."

"Liar. If you're not going to spill, then neither am I." He emphasized the last part like a six-year-old's playground taunt.

They laughed.

"What are you dipshits laughing at?"

"You, Troy, of course." Jesus couldn't help but egg-on the younger man. It was in his genes, and he still wasn't sure if he liked him. "What are you doing here? I didn't see you on the schedule today."

"Just grabbing a few things and checking my appointments tomorrow. If our *amazing* manager were here, I wouldn't have had to come in to do that."

Well, that was one reason not to like the little shit. "What do you have against Stacey? She's the studio manager, not your personal assistant, and she's doing a great job. Any one of us could've checked the schedule for you if you'd called."

"Yeah, but I wouldn't want to bother *artists* at work. The manager should be here for those things."

"It's her *one* day off this week. She does ten times more than the other managers did, and she works twice as many hours as you do. How could you possibly have anything to say in this scenario?"

Troy sputtered for a moment before blurting, "I'm just saying she should be here. Okay? Geez.

Lay off the 'roids man. Chill. It's not that serious." With that illustrious parting statement, Troy disappeared back to his hole—otherwise known as his station.

Jesus turned to ask Dillon if that just happened but stopped when he saw the amused look on his face.

"What?"

"Looks like I got my answer to who you have a crush on." Dillon grinned as he wagged his eyebrows.

"Yeah. I answered you. No one."

"Oh, no. There is no taking it back after what I just witnessed. You came to her proverbial rescue like a knight in shining... muscle car."

"That doesn't mean anything. I would've defended any one of you the same way."

"Mmmhmm. Sure. I completely believe you." Except the fucker shook his head "no" as he spoke.

"Whatever, man. Believe what you want. Stacey and I are not a thing."

Dillon's eyes got wide as saucers. "I said you had a crush on her. Not that you two were a thing. You two are actually a thing? Since when? Damn. I need to come and push your buttons more often. I would've gotten these juicy morsels out of you sooner. Tell me more."

Jesus punched Dillon in the bicep and Dillon snickered like that told him everything he needed to know. The punch was a little harder than "playful", but still much lighter than he really wanted to. He knew Dillon was messing with him. They weren't teenage girls, and Dillon didn't really want the gossip. It still rubbed him the wrong way that even if he wanted to tell Dillon what was going on between him and Stacey, he couldn't because he didn't know, either.

Sleeping with her once had been one thing, but twice? And both times in the studio? He was officially in uncharted territory.

Chapter Seventeen

Stacey

Fingers trembling, she tried to type the code into the keypad, but the door just buzzed at her. Again. Flustered and conflicted, she was both nervous to see Jesus and frustrated that he hadn't just opened the back door for her already. His Chevelle was the only other car in the back parking lot, so she knew he was in there. Clearly, she was having issues, and surely, he could hear the door buzzing over and over. Where was he?

Cursing his name as she tried again, the door opened from the inside and revealed the man himself.

"Hey, there *mariposa*." He stepped aside while holding the door so she could enter. "Did you forget the code? I was checking my schedule at the front desk, or I would've been here sooner."

She sighed at herself. Being frustrated with him was ridiculous. It wasn't his fault. She was just projecting her feelings onto the only other person at work that morning, and maybe she would've projected her feelings on him specifically, anyway.

But who knew?

They walked together to the front desk where he'd left the shop's appointment book open.

"You put me down for a Sailor Jerry consultation today. I guess Jeff didn't tell you that he takes all of those."

"Actually, he told me to give them all to you."

"Huh? Are you sure? That doesn't make any sense. He's amazing at Sailor Jerry tattoos. I'm okay, I guess, but he's better. What appointments is he taking?"

"None."

"What? Why?"

She shrugged her shoulders. She'd thought it was odd too but didn't question it. She figured it wasn't her place to question her new boss.

"I'll catch him later and find out what the fuck he's up to. He mentioned something, but..." Jesus didn't complete the thought like he'd just realized he was speaking out loud. "*Gracias*, Stacey. The appointment book looks good, by the way. You're doing a great job with scheduling. Not that I need to because I'm sure he sees it too, but I'll be sure to mention that to Jeff as well."

Her heart started beating faster, and she was sure her cheeks were red. She took a breath before she responded, so she wouldn't sound like a giddy teenager who just received a compliment from a boy she liked. Even though that was exactly what just happened.

"Thanks, Jesus. That means a lot." *There. That*

was a good response.

With a quick nod, he smiled and began to walk away, but she couldn't let him just yet or she would lose her nerve. She'd been up much too late considering her options with Jesus, and she'd decided sometime in the wee hours of the morning.

"Uh, Jesus?" She cleared her throat and started over. "Drinks? Friday night? You free?" *Wow. That went smoother in my head.*

His smile grew. He really had the best smile.

"I'd love that." He paused. "Somewhere different, though."

She laughed. "Agreed." Neither one of them wanted to run into that crazy waitress again. "Any suggestions?"

"I know just the place. What does your schedule look like that day? I'm here most of the day, but I'm not closing."

"I'm working a shift at the pub that day, but I'm not closing either."

"Okay. Can I pick you up?"

She paused to consider how she felt about that, but made up her mind rather quickly.

"Yes. I'll text you my address. Seven o'clock?"

"Perfect. See you then." He smiled as he walked away, and she almost missed the office chair behind the front desk as she sat down. Luckily, he didn't see that.

She only had a few hours to take care of inventory and a supply order before she had to leave for her shift at the pub, so she hustled to set up her cash drawer for the day. She opened the safe and removed the stacks of bills they used to make change and set it on the desk while she closed the safe. She methodically counted every bill she placed in the drawer and recorded it in the ledger.

After closing and locking the drawer, she placed the key in her pocket for safekeeping while she went to the storage room to take an inventory of their supplies. It wasn't exactly thrilling work, but it was, at least, satisfying work where she wasn't micromanaged. She took pride in doing her job well.

When it was time to head to the pub, she was glad she got everything accomplished, and left the key to the cash drawer in the capable hands of one of the artists. The shop had gone through enough managers in the last year that all the artists knew how to close down the place when she wasn't there. Whoever was the last in the shop would record the bare minimum needed and she would come in the next day to handle the remainder of the tedious paperwork.

Walking into the pub after working at the shop reminded her why she liked working at the pub in the beginning. It was a fun atmosphere and she'd forgotten that over time, the more she worried about bills and getting enough hours to cover those bills.

Technically, the studio paid her enough to be comfortable, but she'd grown attached to the pub and would have a hard time quitting for good. She loved that she could make a living off one job, but could still make a few extra dollars having fun. For the first time in a while, things were looking up.

Her shift at the pub flew by like minutes and kept her mind off her date with Jesus in a few days. If she hadn't been busy, she probably would have worked herself into a frenzy and already called to cancel. Kelsey, her manager, even gave her an excellent excuse when she asked her to work a double on Friday.

She surprised both of them by turning down the offer. She knew if she canceled with Jesus, she'd have a hard time working up the nerve to ask him out again and take the chance she so desperately wanted to take. Maybe he would continue to pursue her like he said he would, but she wanted it to be her decision and not wonder later if he'd just worn her down.

She'd gone from *no way* to unsure to full-blown *yes, I have to,* in less than a week. Even she had to wonder what she was thinking, but she wasn't. She wanted to throw caution to the wind and just *be* for the first time in years. She hadn't given herself permission to live without guarantees in so long that she felt she deserved this one rash decision and just prayed it wouldn't blow up in her face.

Rushing home when her shift was over on Friday, she made a mental list of what to accomplish when she got there. Pick up enough so she didn't look like a slob; shower complete with shaving—all shaving—it had been dark at the studio their first time, and all out frenzied their second time, so she wasn't too self-conscious, but she would be prepared for the next time. She'd try that new eyeshadow thing she'd seen on social media, find *something* to wear, and do it all in less than an hour. Crap. She should have told him eight o'clock, not seven.

She must've changed her outfit eighteen times after doing her makeup three times before she heard the knock on her front door.

"Hold on!" she bellowed, with her fourth pair of pants halfway up her legs.

Buttoning the pants and slipping on her shoes as she hopped to the door, she answered completely out of breath. "Hey."

Dressed in dark gray slacks and a burgundy Henley with his dark wavy hair hanging loose over his shoulders, he looked like he'd stepped off the pages of a magazine. At work, he usually dressed in jeans and t-shirts with his hair either back in a simple ponytail or up in a man-bun. She had to admit that she'd never liked long hair on men and often made fun of man-buns before she met Jesus, but thanks to him, Brock O'Hurn, and Jason Momoa, she was definitely a man-bun convert. Nothing could've prepared her for his casually-dressed-up look though. That was pure, panty-melting hotness.

"*Hola, mariposa.*" He smirked as he took a bold

step in her apartment and threw an arm around her waist, bringing them nose to nose. "Starting without me?"

She smirked back. "And what if I was?"

He groaned and kissed her hard. "That is not how I intended to greet you tonight, but damn, I think you're my dream girl."

She laughed as she pushed him back, so she could turn around and grab her purse. "Gee. I'm so happy to hear that I meet such high standards."

He took her hand and kissed her knuckles as they walked out her front door. "You have no idea." He let that cryptic statement hang in the air as he walked her to his car. She loved his classic muscle car. Growly. Smooth. Dark. Muscular. Without a doubt, a fitting car for him.

He opened her door, and she slid into the buttery soft leather seat. As he drove out of her apartment complex, she asked, "Where are we going?"

"You'll see."

"Hmm. I've never been a fan of those two words."

"Give me a chance to change your mind?"

"Well, okay, but just one. So, use it wisely." She winked at him. She was at least half joking.

He laughed. "I promise to make it count."

Nerves hit her when he aimed his car towards the freeway. Wherever they were going was going to be outside her comfort zone.

"Don't worry, *mariposa.* It's not far, and I

guarantee it's worth it." Taking her hand in his, he brought her fingers to his lips and placed a gentle kiss to reassure her. Amazed at how in-tune he was to her, she could only smile and nod. She was okay. She trusted him. Mostly.

It wasn't long before he pulled up to a restaurant with an open patio on Mission Bay. She'd thought they were going to a bar or club. "I thought this was drinks."

"I know that's what we said, but you've worked all day without much of a break. I thought we could order a little something to munch on with our drinks."

Her heart melted a little more at how considerate he was. He was right. She'd barely had anything to eat all day and her stomach chose that moment to rumble and tell her just how displeased it was about that.

He chuckled. "Sounds like you agree with my choice."

She placed her hand back in his and squeezed. "I do. Thanks."

They smiled at each other for a few beats, and she wondered if he was going to kiss her. She liked his kisses very much.

But he didn't.

"Wait right there." He jumped out of the car and came around to her side. She didn't need a man to open doors for her, but it was nice to be with someone who wanted to. Her door swung open, and he offered his hand as she stepped out of the car. It was the little things that showed her who he was as a person and not just his cocky, confident side that most people saw.

Her musings put another smile on her face as she remembered that he had four sisters. A fact he'd shared during drinks last time they went out. She pictured him as a teenager growing up around all those women and all the female wisdom that they must have imparted upon him. It was no wonder why he was the way he was.

He placed her hand in the crux of his elbow and they walked arm in arm to the hostess stand. That simple act was somehow more intimate than if they'd held hands. She felt safe, protected, close, cherished. Damn, he was turning her into a puddle of goo. She thought she should care more about that, but it was so easy to go with the flow with him—natural even—once she let herself feel the pull that he had on her.

The hostess showed them to a table at the edge of the patio, where they had an uninterrupted view of the bay and the marina. The soft lighting of the restaurant, the boats navigating the bay as they passed, and the early summer breeze off the water made for the perfect setting. She had to admit he'd chosen the location for their date well. Much better than the bar she'd chosen before, even though the circumstances were different. That wasn't supposed to be a date, so the atmosphere never entered her mind, but this was a thousand times better.

Pulling out a chair, he gestured for her to sit down, and she swooned a little more. Their hostess had barely walked away when their server appeared. She ordered a crisp Chardonnay she recognized on the menu, and he ordered his usual Guinness, but they needed a moment to look over the menu before they ordered anything to eat.

"What looks good to you, *mariposa*?"

She looked for a moment. The shrimp ceviche looked amazing, and the calamari sounded good, but she figured he'd rather the wings or nachos. Not that she was against those things, but why come to a restaurant on the water and not get seafood?

"It all looks good. I'm so hungry, I can't choose. What do you think?"

He took a minute to study her, not the menu, and surprised her with his answer. "Well, I haven't had good calamari in forever, but the nachos look good too, if that's more your speed."

"I like calamari."

"Great calamari it is. And maybe the shrimp ceviche too? I figure if you're open to one, you're open to the other and we are at a seafood restaurant."

Hmm. He's a mind reader, too. I wonder if he's also thinking that calamari is an aphrodisiac. I'm certainly not going to bring it up.

She smirked at him. "I was just thinking the same thing." *And then some.*

He reached across the table, laid his hand on

hers and looked into her eyes. "I'm glad we're on the same wavelength. I wonder what else we have in common."

Dear Lord, he really is a mind reader. His words weren't erotic in the slightest, but the way he looked at her was. A spark went straight to her core and lit a small flame. It made her shiver despite the burn.

He quirked an eyebrow. "Cold?"

She shook her head. "No."

He smiled at her answer like he knew the real reason for her shiver, and he probably did. She should have been at least a little embarrassed at her reaction to his innocuous words, but she had a hard time feeling anything but pure attraction and lust around him. Like he'd flipped that switch on in her and there was no turning it off.

Their server returned with their drinks, and Jesus ordered for them. She took a sip of her wine as she thought about what to say. They'd talked about so much the other night that she was at a loss for anything to say. The last thing she wanted was for him to think she was dull. What if all they ever had to say to one another was innuendo?

He reached across the table for her hand. "Hey, you look like you're freaking out a little. If this is too much, we can go. I know it's probably a little… more romantic than you were expecting."

"No. No. It's perfect. I love the atmosphere. It's the exact kind of place I would have picked if I knew it existed, but I don't come out this way very often. Since I moved here, I've stuck close to where I live and work and where my aunt lives. And that's all in about five square miles."

He looked shocked. "San Diego is huge. You haven't tried out all the beaches? The hiking trails? Coronado Island? The mountains? None of that?"

She shook her head. "I'm kind of a homebody. I work a lot, and when I'm not working, I like to relax."

"I can understand that, but I would really love to show you some of my favorite places if you'll let me."

"Sure. I'd like that."

"Great. It's settled. Hiking in the morning, it is."

Her eyes nearly bugged out of her head, and she choked on her wine. "What?"

"I'm kidding! You should see the look on your face."

She pulled her hand from his grasp and scowled at him.

"Hey. I'm sorry. I was just messing around. It would be best first thing in the morning before the sun gets too high in the sky, but we can work up to that."

She rolled her eyes at him, but couldn't help the smirk on her face. "Beaches first."

He laughed. "Okay, beaches first. I can work with that."

Realizing she'd just agreed to spend a lot more time with him should have freaked her out, but it only increased her anticipation. Time with him was like a drug. The more she had, the more she wanted. He was dangerous.

Their amazing food came and went, but their conversation—much like the wine—flowed freely, easily, and endlessly. And again, they found themselves closing the place down.

As she drained the last sip of her wineglass, he asked, "Ready to get out of here?"

She looked around the nearly empty restaurant. "Yeah. I figured our server would have brought the check by now, but I don't see him anywhere."

He smirked, and she swooned a little. It was the wine. "I already paid."

Her eyes shot to his. "What?"

"I already paid. When I went to the restroom, I intercepted him on his way to the table with the bill."

"Oh. I guess that settles that."

"Did you want to pay, *mariposa*?"

"No. 'Want' is a strong word. I *wanted* to spar over who paid before graciously letting you pick up the check." She winked. Again, it was the wine.

He threw his head back and laughed. "Next time, *mariposa*. I promise."

He stood and walked around to her side of the table. Placing his hand on the back of her chair, he leaned down, whispering in her ear from behind. "I guess that means we can get out of here."

The act gave her goosebumps, and her core clinched. Her body all but sang *Yes!*

He pulled her chair out as she stood up and

placed his hand on the small of her back as they walked out of the restaurant. He opened the door to his car, and she nearly stumbled as she lowered herself in. The wine was catching up to her.

They were silent as he drove her home, and she wondered if his thoughts mirrored her own. All she could think about was the moment he walked her to her door. Would he kiss her silly? Would she invite him in? Would he come in if she did? Would they have sex again? Her core clinched at that last thought. She wanted to. She *really* wanted to. But in her inebriated state, she wondered if she was only considering it because her usual inhibitions were down. She sighed. Damn, she almost wished she was more drunk than she was so she could stop overthinking, but she also wanted to remember every moment with him. How had she stopped over-thinking their first time together?

"What's that sigh for, *mariposa*?"

"Just thinking."

"Ahead?" He grinned and winked at her before returning his eyes to the road. That answered her question about whether his thoughts had strayed where hers had.

She laughed. "Yes. Ahead. Back. Up. Down. You name it. All over."

His eyes were softer when he looked back at her like he felt her nerves and understood. Damn, he was good. How did any woman stand a chance when he looked at them like that? Much less, how did *she* stand a chance?

They were back at her apartment complex in record time, or at least, it felt like it. Ever the gentleman, he opened her door and walked her to her apartment on his arm like he'd walked her into the restaurant.

She paused before she put the key in the lock to turn and look at him.

He just grinned and pulled her body flush with his before he dropped his head and kissed her like a starving man. She wrapped her arms around his neck as one of his hands slid into her hair and the other slid down to her ass. She moaned and he slipped his tongue in her mouth. Their dueling tongues and his hardening cock against her stomach turned her brain to mush and made her pants damp. Forget her underwear, those were past soaked through.

Speaking while still trying to kiss her, he said, "Hand me your keys."

She froze for a split second before handing them over, but it was enough for him to notice. He pulled back an inch to study her eyes. His gaze asked if she was sure while his lips held back the words. She nodded and meant it.

He grinned and kissed her hard as he deftly handled the lock on her door. Before she'd realized he had the door open, he was coaxing her legs around his waist and carrying her into her apartment. He kicked the door shut, and she kicked off her heels and dropped her purse while they were still in the foyer.

"Shoes," she said against his lips. He understood and stopped to toe out of his shoes by the front door before heading towards the couch, but she managed an "Uh, uh" against his lips and shook her head. "Bed."

He jerked back in surprise and looked her in her eyes again, but she was sure. Surer than she'd been about anything in a very long time. She'd spent too long being afraid and too long just being a victim of circumstance. She was going to make something happen for herself. It was her decision as much as it was his. It wasn't like she was giving her heart away or anything. Somehow, he'd stopped her from over-thinking again and she was going to follow her gut while it was still louder than her head.

Chapter Eighteen

Jesus

He followed her directions back to her bedroom and crawled on to her bed with her legs still around his waist and every one of her delicious curves pressed firmly against him. The lights were off except for a soft glow from the lamp beside her bed. Between that and the full moon through the window, he had all the light he needed to appreciate her body better than he'd been able to the first time. As he laid her down, his kisses moved from her mouth down to her neck, then her collar and her chest before her shirt got in the way.

He looked up into her eyes again to judge her reaction. When all he saw was lust and eagerness, he sat up a little to grab the hem of her shirt and pulled it over her head.

She laid back on the bed and his eyes went straight to her breasts. In a sheer bra that left absolutely nothing to the imagination, they begged to be worshiped properly. He bent down and sucked a nipple into his mouth, straight through the fabric as his hand pinched the other one. She groaned as she dug her heels into his ass, pushing his cock harder against her center, and they both groaned.

"Fuck. I want you in me. Like, now."

He chuckled as he blew on her wet nipple. "Patience, *mariposa*."

She growled in impatience as she reached for the hem of his shirt and pulled it over his head. The hungry look in her eyes as she drank in his tattooed upper body made the hours under the needle and working out nearly every day completely worth it.

He reached for her bra and pulled the cups down. Her breasts spilled out, finally free from their confines. He loved the whole female body, but there was no doubt in his mind that he was a breast-man, through and through. He grabbed both in his hands and alternated sucking and nipping at her nipples until she was writhing so hard underneath him that he was about to come in his pants from the friction.

Letting go of her breasts—he was going to have to fuck those later—he focused back on her bra, but instead of unhooking it, he pulled it down to her waist. With her arms still through the straps, it restricted her movement from her shoulders to her elbows. Tightening both straps as far as they would go held her elbows even closer to her sides. He'd never tied a woman up in her own bra before, but he loved to experiment in the bedroom.

Taking women to new heights in new ways was practically a hobby of his. Turned out the bra trick wasn't perfect, but it would do. He liked control and sensed she needed to give a little up. He wanted to test how much she would allow him to take and figured actual ropes would freak her out. Not that he had ropes with him anyway.

"What's this?"

"Restraint, *mariposa*. Do you like it?"

She didn't answer, but the hazy need in her eyes said she was already accepting it and reveling in it. She finally bit her lip and nodded. He'd take it. This time.

"Next time, *mariposa*, I'll want to hear 'yes' or 'no'. Understood?"

She nodded again, but all he did was quirk his eyebrow and she added, "Yes. Okay."

She took cues well. He could have a lot of fun with that.

He scooted down between her legs and kissed down her belly until he got to her pants. They were skintight and left little to the imagination, but he was still dying to see what was underneath. Making quick work of the button and zipper, he peeled the offending pants down her thick, toned legs until they were just fabric on the floor.

Goldmine. Behind a sheer thong that matched her bra was the most beautiful, shaved pussy he'd ever seen, glistening with arousal in the soft light. He was sure he'd never described a pussy as "beautiful" before, but hers was. Even better was that there was nothing obstructing his view, and he took a moment to stare his fill. Damn, she was perfect.

She squirmed under his perusal and tried to bring her knees together with him still between her legs. He pushed them back open, wider than before, and ran his finger down the edge of her thong until it disappeared between her ass cheeks and back up again.

"What's the matter, *mariposa*? Don't want me to look?"

She looked unsure of how to answer that, and he realized he was probably pushing her comfort zone a little too far. He took her mind off of it by pulling her thong to the side with one hand and swiping a finger from her dripping pussy to her clit and back again with the other hand. He kept up the pace, each swipe spending a little more time on her clit, over and over until she was clutching the bedsheets by her hips and had completely forgotten her self-consciousness.

Her pussy fluttered and clinched like her orgasm was near, so he leaned down, worked two fingers in her folds, curled them up and down and worked her clit with both his thumb and his tongue until she was screaming his name so loudly that her neighbors would surely look at her funny in the morning.

He kept going until the last of her orgasm faded and looked up to a couple of heavy-lidded eyes staring back at him. He crawled up the bed and kissed her hard and long so she could know how good she tasted.

Pulling back with one last peck, he asked, "How are you feeling, *mariposa*? Tired?"

She shook her head. "Invigorated."

A grin broke out across his face. "Perfect, *mariposa*. Just perfect."

He jumped up and made quick work of his slacks and boxers. He wasn't sure what was hotter: her lying there, post-orgasm, half restrained, or her watching every movement he made as he rolled on a condom.

He stalked back to her like a panther eyeing his prey and climbed back between her legs. Hooking a finger in her thong, he pulled it down and all the way off, and then lined himself up. "If you can keep your arms at your sides, I'll keep you coming all night long. Deal?"

She squirmed around like she could get his dick in her pussy if she just moved close enough. "Ugh. Deal. Now go!"

He smirked as he looked into her eyes and pushed his way in. Then he lowered his head and kissed her soft, but deep once he bottomed out. Kissing and nipping as he went faster and faster. Her hands shot up and touched his sides as much as she could with her elbows still loosely bound to her sides.

"Hands, *mariposa*."

She groaned and grabbed the bedspread like a good girl. "But I want to touch you!"

He chuckled but didn't answer. If she kept touching him, he was going to shoot off like a rocket before he made her come again, and he couldn't have that.

Shifting back, he lifted her legs over his shoulders and picked up the pace and the force.

"Oh. Fuck. Jesus. Fuck. Fuck. Jesus. Fuck." A word every time he thrust in like a chant.

He dropped one of her legs to the side and turned her body just enough to change the angle again, and she moaned deep in her chest. He knew she was close again, so he grabbed one of her hands and encouraged her to touch her own clit.

Her eyes flew open and focused on his. At first, he wasn't sure if she would, but then her fingers started to move against her clit, and with each stroke, she got more confident.

The sight was so erotic, he wasn't sure he could watch without losing his load, but that didn't mean he could look away as she pleasured herself. As her pussy started to flutter around his cock, his own orgasm rushed to the surface. Her flutters got stronger and stronger until she was screaming again just as he spilled over, filling the condom. Kissing her as they both came down from their highs, he loved that she was so vocal and didn't hold back in expressing herself.

Just pulling out of her nearly made him swallow his tongue, as the action touched every nerve ending in his spent cock. He took the condom off and threw it away in her bathroom.

When he returned, she was still lying in the same spot, sated, with sleepy looking eyes. He unhooked the bra still around her waist and arms, and pulled the sheet and bedspread up over her, tucking her into her bed.

Figuring she was nearly asleep, he kissed her goodbye and started to gather his things to let himself out.

"What are you doing?"

"Heading home."

"Stay."

He froze. He never stayed over. It was just a knee-jerk reaction to pack up and leave afterwards.

"Are you sure?"

"Yes. Come here." She held her hand outside the covers he'd just tucked her into, beckoning him over to her.

He dropped his things and climbed into her bed behind her. The big spoon to her little spoon. He couldn't remember the last time he'd cuddled with anyone. It was such an intimate act, even more intimate than sex. Sometimes sex could just be sex, but cuddling was somehow more.

"Are you freaking out?"

He huffed a laugh. "Maybe, a little."

"Don't freak out. This is good."

Easier said than done.

"You said I was special, so don't treat me like I'm not."

Damn. That hit him in the gut. He wrapped his arms tighter around her, pulled her body closer into him, and kissed the side of her head.

"You're right, *mariposa*. You're absolutely right."

She snuggled into him a little more in answer, and he drifted off to sleep thinking of all the ways that she was special to him.

Chapter Nineteen

Stacey

She woke up alone, wondering if it'd all been a dream. Sitting up and realizing she was naked, she pulled the sheet up to her chest and conceded it couldn't have all been a dream. But maybe she dreamt the part where he climbed into bed with her and slept next to her.

Just as she'd convinced herself she was all alone in her apartment, Jesus, dressed only in the slacks he'd worn the night before, walked into her room with two cups of coffee and handed her one as he sat on the bed next to her.

"I thought I heard you stirring in here. I hope you don't mind. I made myself at home." His ever-present smirk said he knew she didn't mind, and all her apprehension flew out the window.

"You're here."

His smile fell. "Yeah. You asked me to stay."

She buried her face in her hands. "Oh my god. I did, didn't I?"

"Do you want me to go?" He stood up and she

177

latched onto his arm, almost spilling both of their coffees.

"No." He looked confused. "I'm just embarrassed that I begged you to stay when you wanted to leave."

"It's not that I wanted to. I just thought I was supposed to. I don't... I haven't usually... in the past. Stayed. But you were right. I told you that you were special, and then I didn't treat you any differently."

"Fuck. I said that too. I blame the wine. I'm not usually so forward. Or blatant." She frowned at what he must think of her.

He leaned over and kissed her over their coffees. "Hey, no frowning. You were right. My actions didn't match my words, and I'm sorry."

Wow. A man who could apologize. A rare breed indeed. She still had a small voice in her head calling her needy. It sounded awfully like her mother.

"Can I make it up to you? With a beach you've never seen, perhaps?"

She opened her mouth to answer just as her phone rang in the other room.

"I'll get it." He hopped up to retrieve her phone and returned while it was still ringing.

Surprised to see Kelsey calling, she answered right before it went to voicemail as she set her coffee mug on the bedside table. "Hello."

"Stacey! Thank God you picked up. Jan quit. I need you to work a double and close tonight."

The first time she'd received a phone call like that, she thought it meant the end of fighting for adequate hours at the pub, only to realize "quitting" was something Jan did when she wanted the weekend off at the last minute. Even after she knew better than to believe Jan quit, she still took the last-minute shifts because the extra money never hurt.

Thanks to her new job at the studio, though, she felt like she had a choice for the first time in forever.

"I don't know, Kelsey. I have plans today."

"What? Are you kidding?"

"No. I'm not." She could understand Kelsey's surprise. She'd never hesitated to take on shifts before.

"I really need you to work tonight or we'll be short staffed. Everyone else is either already working or has already turned down the hours." Meaning Kelsey waited to call her last. Lovely.

She sighed. "I'll call you back and let you know."

"Umm. Okay."

She hung up without saying "bye" and threw herself back on the bed in frustration. She realized she was still naked when her breasts spilled out the top of the sheet, putting them on full display, and she wasn't alone. As she reached to pull the sheet up, Jesus reached to pull it all the way off her body, and he was quicker, even with a coffee mug still in his hand.

She squeaked. "What do you think you're doing?

I'm cold!"

"Let me help with that." Covering her body with his, he leaned down and kissed her long and languidly. It wasn't until she was about to pass out that she remembered to breathe through the kisses.

He took a breast in each hand. *Where did his coffee go?* "Last night, I told myself that I would fuck these soon."

That sent a shiver through her as he continued to knead her breasts and play with her nipples. One of his hands moved from her breast to her clit as he slid down her body. He sucked a nipple into his mouth, and then said, "So who was on the phone?"

Was he serious? Her brain was already mush.

He bit her nipple, and she yelped. The sharp pain turned into a delicious ache, and she learned something about herself when his finger swirled in the copious wetness at her core and brought it up to her clit.

Threading her fingers through his hair at the back of his head, she subconsciously held him in place as he played her body like his favorite instrument. Minutes passed as he split her focus between the suction on her nipple and the vibrations on her clit before he spoke again. "The call, *mariposa*."

"Ugh."

He chuckled. "Trust me, *mariposa*. Tell me. I'm a great listener." He was still grinning as he took her nipple back in his mouth. He slipped one finger inside her and then another as he continued his ministrations on her clit with his thumb.

Strung out and so close to the edge, she groaned as she rushed the words out in one breath. "It was Kelsey. She wanted me to come in tonight."

"Hmm. And do you want to?" He curled his fingers inside her and found a spot that made her eyes roll back in her head.

She groaned louder. How was she supposed to think under such conditions?

"Don't think, *mariposa*. Just feel. How do you feel? Do you want to take the shift?"

"Ugh. No. Fuck them. She only. Called me. Because. She was. Desperate." Her words were punctuated by her quick breaths.

"Now come for me."

His fingers went faster and faster on her clit as he bit her nipple again, and she shattered. "Oh, Jesus!"

While stroking her through the orgasm all the way to the end, he kissed his way from her breast to her mouth.

She wrapped her arms around his neck and deepened the kiss, hungry for a taste of him. Their tongues clashing and dancing until they were breathless. His kisses had a way of making her lightheaded, so when he broke the kiss to say something, she had to ask him to repeat himself.

"What are your plans today?"

"Huh? I don't have any plans."

He gave her a confused look. "You told Kelsey

you had plans."

"Oh." She could feel her face heating up in a blush. "I was hoping to make plans with you."

He smirked and she grew more embarrassed before he said, "Me too. So how about that beach, *mariposa*?"

"Umm… rain check?"

His eyebrows furrowed for a moment before his face went blank. She envied his ability to hide what he was thinking. She always wore her thoughts right on her face.

"Okay. Sure." He paused long enough to kiss her on her nose and move to get off her bed. "I'll call you later, then?"

He misunderstood. She was terrible at communicating. Before he could walk out of her bedroom, she started rambling. "It's just that I feel like I just got a free day off when I would have taken that shift, and I'd really love to just chill and binge watch some bad reality TV all day. Want to join me? And you can show me some of the adventures I'm missing another day?"

She phrased the last statement like a question because she didn't feel like either of them knew if there would be another day, but his smile told her that it had been the right thing to say.

"I'd love to, *mariposa*. Give me an hour to run home and shower, and then I'm all yours."

Those words sent tingles up her spine and straight to her traitorous heart. She was glad he was going home for a minute for her to put her head on straight and remind herself that they were just having a bit of fun and seeing where their chemistry led. No hopes. No promises. Just blindly taking a path least traveled—for her anyway.

Thinking about how often he did the things to other girls that he'd done to her was enough to send her anxiety through the roof. She was practically naïve compared to him. She became torn between comparing herself to him and every girl he'd ever been with, and also being super fucking grateful because *holy shit*, he was amazing. Kinky even, and she blushed, realizing how much she'd loved his kink. She was in *so* much trouble.

By the time he returned, she'd showered and dressed in leggings and a top long enough to cover her ass.

His eyes traveled the length of her body when she opened the door. "As much as I'd hoped you'd greet me at the door naked, leggings are definitely almost as good."

He winked at her, and she giggled. Fucking giggled. Who was she?

"The top is going to have to go though. I want to see you."

She looked down at one of her favorite shirts and thought for a moment. She wasn't about to bend over backwards to satisfy his demands, but she could compromise. She grabbed the bottom hem of the shirt in one hand and tied it in a knot at her waist like she'd done as a kid.

She lifted her chin and gave him a defiant grin.

He just chuckled as he walked into her apartment.

They spent the day laughing at stupid people on TV and making out on the couch. She'd worried once they had sex that was all he'd want to do when they were alone, but he didn't hint once that he wanted to go any further. She was both glad and confused.

When he pulled away again after their fourth or fifth hot-and-heavy moment, she had to ask, "What is the problem?" It came out in a yell and his eyebrows nearly hit his hairline. She hadn't meant it to come out so harshly, but her emotions were all over the place.

"There's no problem, *mariposa*."

"Then why aren't we in the bedroom right now?" She hadn't meant to be that blunt, either.

He smirked. *Damn him*. "I'm just taking my cues from you, *mariposa*. The longer we make out, the more tense you become until your mind is either a million miles away or you're thinking way too hard about what we're doing. Whatever is happening is stressing you out. Want to talk about it?"

Damn him again. She was stressed out and she knew she was terrible at hiding it, but she shook her head *no,* anyway.

He sat back on the couch and patted his lap. "Give me your feet."

"What?"

"You heard me. Give me your feet."

Confused by the sudden subject change, she sat

back and reluctantly followed orders.

He started massaging her right foot and *oh my God, those hands.* He hit all the right places with just the right amount of pressure.

"What is this for?"

"I'm relaxing you. Talk to me. Tell me what's going on in that head of yours." He smirked, and to her surprise, she relaxed a fraction.

Chapter Twenty

Jesus

He listened as she started talking.

"I don't really date. I don't know how to do this."

"Neither do I, *mariposa*."

"But you want to?"

"I'm still here. I'm never still here."

"That doesn't answer my question."

"Yes, *mariposa*, I want you. I want to leave my comfort zone for you. It feels right."

"It does, and that's what worries me."

"What do you mean?"

"I need to show you something." She got up and went to her bedroom. He heard a drawer opening and closing before she walked back to the couch and sat down next to him.

Looking down at the item in her hand, she paused before handing a photograph of a young girl to him. He was confused but patient as he waited for Stacey to explain the picture of the girl who was clearly related to her.

With tears in her eyes, she said, "This is my daughter."

He tried, but he couldn't hide his shock. A kid? He looked around the apartment, expecting to see signs a child lived there, but he also knew she lived in a one-bedroom. It didn't make sense.

"You won't find her things around here. I haven't seen her in seven years. I get pictures and updates from her parents, but I didn't even know her name until their first letter about a year after she was born. I got pregnant when I was seventeen. Then I was abandoned by the father, then my parents, and then my friends soon after. Then I abandoned her and ran away to San Diego. That's my story in a nutshell. I thought you should know. I'll understand if you want to leave and forget every wonderful thing you've ever said to me."

Wait. What? He had whiplash from how fast that turned.

Wrapping an arm around her shoulders, he pulled her over until her head rested on his chest. "Back up, *mariposa*. First, I'm sorry about your family and friends. They're crazy. Clearly. Second, I'm not going anywhere, no matter what you tell me. But I do wish you'd fill in more of that story."

"Which part?"

He chuckled and kissed the top of her head. "Tell me about her parents."

"Linda and Ross? They're great. Basically, everything I wish my parents had been. I even flat-out asked them what they'd do if she made a stupid, life-altering mistake like I did. They said that they'd do everything in their power to help her make good choices, and if they'd stopped there, I would've moved on to the next couple. Because that was my parent's argument. That they'd 'raised me right' so the 'failing' was my own to deal with. But Linda and Ross didn't stop there. They continued and said that children weren't mistakes, even when unexpected, and that they would love her and support her through anything she faced. They saw me, not just the baby growing inside me, and understood what I needed to know to let go without fear."

"So, you didn't abandon her. You found her the best parents and left her in their loving care."

"Yeah. I guess." Though she didn't sound convinced, or maybe she wasn't convinced that he was convinced.

"How exactly did you end up in San Diego, then?"

"My dad's sister. She's an artist out here, and the only family that I still speak to. I didn't know much about her until I moved here. My family thinks they're royalty just because we've owned some land for a while, and therefore are entitled to look down on or shun any who they deem 'less than'. Aunt Brenda is a free spirit and rejected everything our family wanted for her. My dad and grandparents like to pretend she doesn't exist, but that's also how I knew she'd help me when I called.

I didn't expect her to bring me all the way here, shelter me and feed me until I figured out my future, but I would say it's all worked out."

She looked up at him, and he smiled before kissing her. "I would say so too, *mariposa*."

"So that's my tragic little story. What can I say? Take me as I am."

He pulled her a little tighter to ward off the lingering ghosts of her past. "I'm sorry you went through all that, *mariposa*, but it also helped shape who you are. And in case I haven't been clear, I really like who you are."

She giggled, and he was so in love with that sound.

∞ ∞ ∞

They stayed in all day. The TV was on, but with their attention on each other, they didn't watch much of it. Instead, they talked. And talked. Some small talk, but mostly real talk. By the end of the day, Stacey knew more about him than probably anyone else on the planet. They shared their childhoods. All the good, bad and ugly of growing up. He told her all about his sisters. They were Ari, short for Ariana; Luci, short for Luciana; Mari, short for Marisol; and Nat, short for Natalia.

"What? Not 'Nati'?" Stacey paused. "Wait. No, I see why. That sounded different in my head."

They both laughed.

Since she shared her experience getting to San Diego, he shared his too. Leaving everything he knew in life, traveling halfway across the country, and being tested more than he'd ever been tested before. Their stories weren't the same, but they were awfully similar.

When evening came, he had to extricate himself and head into the studio for a few hours. He tried to work as few Saturdays as possible, but he was going in at the request of a regular client who was only in town at certain times.

He walked in the backdoor and right into Derrick.

"Watch it! Did you go blind, Jesus? That would explain your linework."

"Fuck you, Derrick. What crawled up your ass?"

Derrick just scoffed and walked away. *What the fuck?*

He didn't have time to dwell on Derrick's mood swings because his client walked through the door.

"Hey man," he greeted his client, "come on back, and we'll get started."

As they walked past the front desk, he wished he'd been able to convince Stacey to come into the studio with him, but she hadn't wanted to. They did need to discuss if they were going to let their coworkers know about their relationship first.

During the tattoo, his phone rang. It was on vibrate, so he didn't check it until it rang again. That time, he glimpsed his sister's name. Arianna.

It wasn't weird to get a phone call from his family, but two was unnerving. He wasn't at a stopping point in the tattoo though, so when he didn't pick that call up either, his sister followed it up with a text, telling him to call her when he could.

The text was better than a third phone call, but not by much. He stayed focused on the task at hand and still delivered his best work for his client. But the moment the appointment was over, he was out the back door for a little privacy to return his sister's call.

"Hello." One word and he knew something was very wrong by the hitch in her voice. Arianna was his oldest big sister, and the one he lovingly referred to as "the bossy one". She was self-assured in all circumstances. Nothing phased her, except for whatever she was about to tell him.

"Hey Ari, what's happening?"

"It's Mia. She hasn't felt well recently, so I took her to the doctor. They ran some tests, and they think it's leukemia. The doctor is supposed to get back to me about our next steps, but I thought you should know."

That was his sister. Straight forward. To the point. Never mind his brain basically hit the brakes somewhere around "leukemia".

He was speechless. Of all the things he thought she might say, that was not even in the realm of possibilities.

"Jesus? Are you there?"

"Yeah." His voice croaked, so he cleared his

throat. "Yeah, Ari. I'm here. Just surprised."

Her laugh was completely devoid of humor. "Surprised. That's one word for it."

"How are you, sis? What can I do?" Was that a stupid question? What do you ask in times like these?

"I'm... scared, and I don't know what anyone can do." His sister sounded smaller than he'd ever heard her. She always knew what to do.

"She's going to be okay, Ari."

"You don't know that. This is not a boo-boo I can sing '*Sana sana colita de rana. Dame un besito para hoy y mañana*' to and she be miraculously all right again." She sounded almost panicked.

"You're right. A nursery rhyme will not make things better, but what about faith? *Papi* is always preaching about faith and claiming the outcome we want. Well, I have faith that she'll respond to whatever treatment the doctors prescribe, and I'm claiming her healing."

She sighed loud enough for him to hear through the phone, but her voice came through in a whisper. "What if my faith isn't big enough?"

"It is, but when you feel like it isn't, the rest of the family and I are here to bolster it."

She was silent for a moment. "You're right. I'm being a defeatist, and that's not who I am. Thank you, Jesus. You want to know what you can do for us? Be our cheerleader. We're going to need it."

"I will, Ari. You can count on it."

They ended the call, and he got in his car to go

home. He didn't need anything back in the studio, and he had no more tattoos scheduled for the rest of the day. He just couldn't handle the questions he'd get for running out the door so quickly.

Chapter Twenty-one

Jesus

"You made it! Come in, you two." Stacey's aunt Brenda was a small, white-and-pink-haired woman. Not small like frail, but small like a spitfire you wouldn't expect could lift canvases bigger than she was. He'd met her a few times, but this was the first time they'd come to one of her parties together.

"Hey, Brenda." He grunted as she pulled him into a bearhug. "Thanks for having us. Stacey says your parties are unlike anything else."

Stacey's eyes got huge, and Jesus winked at her over Brenda's head. Really, she'd said that this was less a party and more of a ploy to attend their own interrogation.

It was the end of spring in San Diego, which meant the days were getting warmer, but there was still a comfortable chill in the evenings. Perfect for opening windows and patio doors during a party, and Brenda had a first-floor apartment that opened to a courtyard, making her modest apartment seem like a sprawling space.

Brenda pointed them towards the bar for a drink so she could greet another couple who came to the door behind them, and they both breathed a sigh of relief that at least when the interrogation started, they'd have drinks in their hands.

"Hey sweetie, what can I get you?" The bartender was a handsome man who clearly knew his way around a bar and apparently knew Stacey too. Even after weeks of dating, he had to resist the caveman urge to wrap his arm around her and claim her as his woman in front of the competition. If he was the type to roll his eyes, he'd be rolling his eyes at himself. He needed to get a grip.

"Hey Tony. I'll have a gin and tonic." She turned her attention to him because it was his turn to tell *Tony* what he wanted to drink and nearly caught him glaring at the man.

"I'll have whatever beer you have available in a bottle."

"Heineken good?"

"Yeah."

He popped the top off the beer and mixed Stacey's drink, and as he handed over their drinks, Stacey introduced them.

"Tony, this is my boyfriend, Jesus. Jesus, this is Tony. He's the regular bartender that Aunt Brenda hires and a good friend." She emphasized the word "friend". For his benefit or Tony's? He wasn't sure, but he could guess he wasn't as good at hiding his impulses as he thought he was.

He extended his hand across the bar to Tony and shook it. "Nice to meet you."

"Great to meet you too, man." Then he turned his attention back to Stacey. "What's this guy got that I haven't got?"

Jesus bristled at the question and opened his mouth to respond on her behalf, but she responded first.

"He likes girls." He was not expecting her to say that though.

"Hey, I like girls."

"Not as much as boys."

He hummed a little. "True." Then, he winked at Jesus, and that broke the ice. They all laughed.

He gave in to the temptation and pulled Stacey to his side. "Sorry, man, I'm taken." Then he winked back.

Tony's initial shock was short-lived before he grinned. "Oh, hold tight to this one, sweetie. He's trouble." The way he said it sounded like a compliment.

"Don't I know it." The way she responded did not. He smacked her ass as punishment, sending Tony into another fit of laughter.

"What's so funny? What did I miss?" Aunt Brenda asked as she came up next to them at the bar.

Tony was the first to answer. "These two are just the cutest. I can't even with them."

"Aren't they?" Brenda turned to him with an earnest look. "Jesus, how is your niece? Mia? I hope you don't mind. Stacey told me about her diagnosis. How is she doing?"

"Oh, of course, that's fine. She's okay. Well, as good as can be expected, I guess. They started the chemo treatments, and they think they caught it in the early stages. So, that's good. Now, we wait and see."

"Well, you let me know if I can do anything. Maybe if she has a benefit, I could donate one of my works to be auctioned off."

"*Gracias*, Brenda. I don't know if they will, but I appreciate the offer. I'll definitely pass it on to my sister."

"Wonderful! Now." She clasped her hands together. "Come with me while I show you off to all my friends."

"Aunt Brenda, he is not a piece of meat!"

Pulling Stacey close to him, he whispered in her ear. "But I'm your piece of meat. *Sucia*."

He nibbled on her ear; she blushed furiously, and he smirked. He loved how responsive she was to his touch, and whispering "dirty" in her ear never hurt.

Brenda snickered. "Okay. Before you two escape my party to do more of... that, mingling first."

So, they mingled. They mingled like they'd never mingled before... and then they went home... exhausted.

∞ ∞ ∞

Stacey

"You wanted to come back to the house tonight. Right?"

She laughed. "Is that a real question? You're already halfway there."

He looked over for a second and smiled at her before returning his eyes to the road. "I'd still take you home if you wanted me to."

She placed her hand on his resting on the gearshift. "Take me home, babe."

He picked up her hand and brought it to his lips. "My pleasure, *mariposa*."

When they exited the car in the driveway, they could already hear the guys having a great time in the backyard.

"Out of the frying pan and into the fire."

"Don't worry, *mariposa*. I'll protect you."

"Gee. I'm so relieved."

He smacked her ass for her sarcasm, and that was exactly why she did it. She giggled and ran into the house. He caught her in the entryway, caged her against the wall with his body, and sipped at her lips.

"Hey, get a room!"

Jesus smiled into the kiss before kissing her harder, and she moaned. Their audience be damned.

BJ laughed and left them alone.

Jesus grabbed her hand as he pulled away. "Come on, *mariposa*. Let's go say hi to everyone."

She groaned. "Tease."

"You started it with that sass."

They walked out to the backyard hand in hand.

"Oh, look! They came up for air."

"You jealous, Beej? This is called a woman. You might find one if you stopped playing with your tool from time to time."

BJ gave Jesus the finger as everybody laughed.

Jesus grabbed a couple of beers as they sat in empty seats around the firepit with his roommates.

"So, BJ. Speaking of your tools." Adam chuckled. "How is the garage doing?"

"Oh, it's great. Cars with mysterious problems. Parts on back-order. Customers who are impossible to please. Just. Great."

"Are you thinking of giving it up?" Jesus sounded worried.

BJ paused, like he was thinking about it. "Nah. I love it too much."

"Oh yeah, I'm feeling all the love." War had a point.

"Just a rough few days." He held up his beer. "This helps."

Will turned to War. "What about you, War? I must miss all the good bodyguard stories, not living here anymore."

"Stories? From War? The man who grunts more than he speaks?"

"Fuck you, Jesus."

"No, thank you." Jesus winked at her, and she

laughed at them all.

She'd spent plenty of nights just like that around the firepit with the guys, and it never got boring.

Jesus stood and held his hand out to Stacey. "Are you ready for bed, *mariposa*?"

She placed her hand in his and let him lead her away from the firepit. "Night, boys."

They walked in the house, and Jesus shut the backdoor on their whistles and catcalls. "So immature."

"Oh yeah, and we're grownups." She smirked at him as she backed up down the hallway.

He stalked after her. "Mmmhmm. Now, where were we, *mariposa*?"

She pointed to her lips and then traced her finger down her neck. "I think you were right about here."

He chased her as she walked faster towards his room, and they were laughing when he tackled her to the bed.

As his body landed on hers, he dipped his head to sip at her lips. His hands caressed her neck, across her collar, down her sternum, and over her breasts. His gentle, slow perusal of her body surprised her. The way he'd pushed her against the wall earlier, she expected him to go hot and heavy once they got to the bed.

"You astonish me, *mariposa*. You're so strong and smart, but humble about it. You don't talk down to anyone even when you can dance circles around them."

She smiled up at him and nuzzled his nose with hers. "Thank you, but I think you mixed some metaphors there."

"See? So smart." They both laughed.

He took his time removing her clothes one piece at a time. His kisses followed his hands as he went until she was naked and so sensitive to his touch that every inch of her skin was an erogenous zone.

He stood up from the bed and stripped slowly, revealing the intricate artwork that covered most of his body. His muscles bunched, bulged and stretched as he lifted his shirt over his head. The perfect-teethed, panty-melting grin that used to piss her off now made her hot all over.

She licked her fingers and touched herself, playing with her clit as Jesus unbuttoned and unzipped his jeans. Stepping out of his pants, he palmed his cock over his briefs and stroked himself while he watched her.

"So sexy, *mariposa*. I could come just watching you."

"We should try that sometime."

"You're on."

He finally pushed his briefs down and his long, fat cock slapped his abs. No matter how many times they'd been together, she never tired of the sight of him naked. It was a glorious view.

Laying his body back over hers, he kissed her slowly as he rubbed his dick over her clit and played with her nipples. Every time he pinched, she felt it in her core, compounding the feel of his thrusting hips against her. She ran her hands over his powerful arms, looped her arms around his neck, and dug her fingers into his luscious hair.

The flared head of his cock found her entrance and he pushed his way inside. She exhaled an involuntary moan, like there wasn't enough room left in her body to take a deep breath. They'd nixed condoms weeks ago after a lengthy discussion about history and consequences.

Best. Decision. Ever.

Maybe it was the lack of condoms, or maybe it was the man, but she'd never felt like this.

The lack of a physical barrier didn't just increase the pleasure, but it brought down her emotional barriers, too. Jesus set a slow rhythm that rocked her in more ways than one. This wasn't just sex, it was making love, and he never stopped kissing her like her tongue held secrets he had to know.

Every thrust lit her up. She was human fireworks. He sat up, lifting her ass with his hands, and she planted her feet on the bed beside his knees. The change in angle made her see stars. If she was fireworks before, this was the grand finale.

"I'm going to come."

"Do it, *mariposa*. Come for me."

A few strokes of her finger over her clit and she flew over the edge into an impossibly long orgasm.

Jesus laid back over her. His movements became erratic as he kissed her and came inside her.

He kissed her languidly as their heart rates slowed and their breathing returned to normal.

The moment was so perfect she wanted to remember it forever, but feelings she couldn't name left her lightheaded.

They were barreling towards a real future together, and she was both excited and terrified.

Chapter Twenty-two

Stacey

It began like any other summer day. She went through the same opening procedures she always did. Only this time, when she removed the change from the safe in Jeff's office to put in the register drawer, she noticed the deposit she'd prepared the night before was open.

She distinctly remembered taping it shut because there were so many bills in the envelope that it wouldn't stay closed. They'd had a particularly good sales day the day before and the deposit had been larger than usual. Curious, she removed it from the safe and recounted it. Five hundred dollars short. How was that possible? She'd been the last one at the studio the night before and the first one in this morning, or at least she thought she was.

Still racking her brain about what could've happened, she didn't hear anyone else come in until they were right behind her.

"*Hola, mariposa.*"

She jumped, and her heart rabbited in her chest. "Jesus."

He smirked. "Sorry I scared you, but I gotta admit that I love when you curse my name."

She swatted his arm. "Stop. This is serious. Does the safe record who opens it and when?"

He furrowed his brow. "No, *mariposa*. I've told Jeff that we should upgrade, but we haven't gotten around to it. Why?"

"The deposit is short. I counted it myself last night and recorded it in the ledger. Today though, I was getting the change to set up the drawer and noticed it was open, so I counted again. It's five hundred dollars short compared to last night."

"Are you serious? So... What? We have a thief?"

She shrugged. She didn't want to outright start accusing people, especially the co-workers she'd only known for a few months.

"That's jumping to a conclusion that I'd rather not entertain yet."

"Right. Good. Yeah."

"Give me a minute to recount and look around. When I'm absolutely sure, we can pull the footage from the cameras."

She pulled everything out of the safe, not that they kept much in there. Just the cash for the drawer, some extra change in case they ran out of pennies or something, and the previous day's deposit, which Jeff would take to the bank the next business day usually.

She spent half an hour double checking

everything meticulously, the sales for the day, confirming which ones were paid by credit and cash, and determining again that the amount of cash she should've had and the cash she actually had were five hundred dollars off. Everything matched what she'd recorded the night before. The bank deposit slip she filled out to save Jeff time even had the correct amount on it. There was no denying it. Someone had taken the money. *But why not all of it?*

Jesus came up behind her and put a reassuring hand on her shoulder. "What did you find, *mariposa*?"

"Same thing I found when I got here. Five hundred dollars missing."

"Damn."

"Yeah."

Leaning over her shoulder, he logged into Jeff's computer and then into the program that ran the cameras. As it was loading, Jeff walked into the office. After one look at their serious faces, he closed the door behind him and asked, "What's wrong?"

Jesus relayed the story of their morning so far.

"Stacey, can you give me and Jesus a minute alone?"

She looked back and forth between them. Jesus seemed as surprised as she was. "Oh. Uh. Sure."

Leaving the office, she wondered what Jeff wanted to say that he couldn't say in front of her. Did he think she did it? It wouldn't make any sense for her to report an amount and then steal from that amount. If she was going to steal, which she never would, she would've altered the books, so it didn't look like anything was missing. But maybe that was precisely why he suspected her. Maybe he thought it was actually genius to steal after the fact thinking she'd be the first cleared of any wrongdoing.

Thinking in circles just gave her a headache and solved nothing. While Jesus and Jeff looked over the footage, she went to the front desk and started her day like normal by checking the day's schedule, then the studio email account and voicemail. Even after returning messages and setting some appointments, the guys hadn't come out of the office, so she started a new supply order and fielded a few more phone calls and emails.

"Stacey, would you come to the office, please?" She hadn't even noticed Jeff's office door open, but his calm invitation did not leave a good feeling in her stomach.

"Coming."

Jesus sat at the computer and barely spared her a glance before turning back to the screen cued to a clip of security footage. Jeff stood behind his chair and gestured for her to sit in the other chair situated next to Jesus so she could see the screen up close and personal. The rock in her belly that had been there all morning grew bigger.

Jeff closed the door once she was seated and instructed Jesus to start the video. It was immediately clear why they were acting so formally with her. The person walking in the back door on the video could've been her. Even she wondered what she was doing on screen, thinking maybe they pulled footage from the wrong night until Jesus switched to another video feed as the figure moved through the studio straight to Jeff's office. The person clearly knew where they were going. They were also able to get not only into the studio, but into Jeff's office and the safe as well.

"You think this is me?" She understood. She did. The images were damning. But she was also hurt. She couldn't help it. Didn't they know her better than that? Maybe Jeff didn't, but Jesus certainly did. Didn't he?

She looked back and forth between them, hoping for a glimmer from either one that they would believe it wasn't her.

"It looks like you. They're wearing your hoodie. They used your code to get in the backdoor. It's bad, *mariposa*." Jesus had some nerve.

If looks could kill, he would be dust. "Don't say that to me and then call me that. I shouldn't have to defend myself to you. I promise I wasn't here last night, and I lost that hoodie a week ago. I don't know how this person got my code, but lots of people look the same on security footage in an oversized black hoodie."

"You're right. This isn't proof of anything other than the fact that someone stole from us. Without this video, I would have no reason to suspect you,

Stacey. You've done an amazing job here so far." Jeff took a deep breath before continuing. "Which is why I will not fire you or even suspend you. You will, however, be on a very short leash. Everyone will, in fact. Frankly, I'm proceeding as if you're all thieves. Maybe that's unfair, but so is firing someone without proof. Do you agree?"

She nodded, but what exactly was she agreeing to? The fact that firing her would be unfair? Yes. She agreed wholeheartedly. Going back to square one of trust? That wasn't ideal where Jeff was concerned, but Jesus's lack of faith in her just made her angry.

"Good, because I want you to keep this between us for now. I don't want to tip off the actual thief or alarm the others. We'll just tell everyone it's time to make some changes." Jeff switched his focus from her to Jesus. "We've let things go for too long. It's time to have some checks and balances around here. Stacey may not be our thief, but we do have one."

She flinched when Jeff said, "may not be", and Jesus noticed but still continued to say nothing. The longer she sat in that office with the two of them, the more his betrayal sunk into her bones. She needed to get out of there.

"Am I free to go? There's a lot to do before I have to leave for my shift at Kelly's."

"Sure. Just don't forget what I said. This issue doesn't leave this office."

"Got it."

No way in hell she'd be chatting with her coworkers any time soon. She didn't know who framed her and until she could fake any niceties, she'd speak to them as long as it pertained to the job and that was it.

She put her head down and finished the supply order she'd started earlier and a few other tasks while dealing with customers and making appointments. She'd nearly made it to the end of her shift home free when Jesus came to the front desk.

He looked properly humbled, but she wasn't interested in how *he* felt. Just how he'd made her feel.

"Can we talk before you leave?"

"Is it about how you don't trust me? Or how you accused me of stealing?" She was glad no one was around, considering she'd agreed not to tell anyone else in the shop.

"You know that's not true."

"I thought I did, but that's not what happened in that office."

He hung his head. "I'm sorry it looked that way, but you think I didn't try to convince Jeff it wasn't you? Why do you think it took so long for him to call you into the office? We found the footage immediately and then fought over it. He thinks I'm blind where you're concerned, but at least he agreed to give you a chance to clear your name."

"That might not be worse than being fired, but it's almost as bad. Now I have to prove that I'm a trustworthy employee, but what have I been doing for the last few months? I have to prove something didn't happen, which is a million times harder than proving something *did* happen. Meanwhile, someone here actively hates me enough to frame me, and to top it off, my boyfriend is the one questioning me like an actual thief."

The more she spoke, the more his face fell. *"Mariposa…"*

"No. Not right now. If I don't leave now, I'll be late for my shift. I have to go."

She left without another word, breaking her own heart further than he had in the process. She didn't know where they would go from there, but she had to focus on clearing her name. Then she could decide if she cared to continue things with Jesus.

Chapter Twenty-three

Jesus

What a shitty day. He wished he'd been able to convince Stacey that he was on her side, but she didn't want to hear any of it. By the time he got home that night, she still wasn't answering his calls or texts. He knew she was probably still at Kelly's, but the pub was slow enough on Wednesday nights that she could have answered if she wanted to. He certainly wasn't going to drop by and make trouble for her at her other job. No. He was sentenced to go home and quietly stew until she would speak to him. At least none of his roommates were around to ask him about his crummy mood. He wouldn't have been able to handle that.

Collapsing on the couch and turning on a sitcom, he got lost in mindless rerun after rerun and tried not to think about the fact that his phone wasn't ringing. He didn't know how long he'd sat there. Just that it was dark when he got home and light when his phone finally rang.

He fumbled his phone trying to pick it up, nearly missing the call, and tried not to sound disappointed when he picked up his sister's call.

"Hey, Luci. What's the matter?" Luciana was his second oldest sister, and if Ari was the bossy one, then Luci was her second in command. They were only a year apart, and both had been raised to help care for the younger three siblings. Luci was a pediatrician in Dallas, and it was she who prompted Ari to ask Mia's doctor to look again at Mia's seemingly mundane symptoms.

"Why do you assume that something's wrong?"

"Because you've never been one to call and chat, and you certainly wouldn't be calling at," he checked the time on his phone, "six thirty in the morning." Not that he and his sister never spoke, she just preferred texting to phone calls, and he was more than okay with that.

"Well, nothing drastic has changed, so I'm sorry I worried you. But I am calling for a reason."

"And?" She'd paused, and it wasn't like her to be timid to say something.

"I think you need to come home for a bit."

"What? Why? I thought there wasn't anything I could do."

"I think you underestimate how much you could do just by being here. No one else knows I'm calling, and I'm not telling you that you must come home. But we miss you, and we need to come together as a family right now. We could use the morale boost that you always provide, especially Mia."

And that was how he ended up on a flight from

San Diego to Houston just after noon that day.

He'd called Jeff and woke him up to explain what was happening, and then he'd called the studio. He left a message—that Stacey would probably get—asking someone to call and cancel his appointments and not to schedule anything else until he got back.

Adam emerged from his room as Jesus was hanging up with the studio. His hair messed like he fell asleep at his desk again. "Hey. What's this about canceling appointments? You're going somewhere?"

"Yeah. I spoke to my sister this morning. I'm going home for a little while. My family needs me."

"Did something change with your niece?"

"No. Not really. But she needs her *tio*. I should've gone when I first got the news, but I had hearts in my eyes and didn't want to leave Stacey."

"And now?"

"And now... Now, Stacey's not speaking to me anyway, but if she was, I hope she's the kind of girl who understands that sometimes you just do what you have to for family."

Adam clapped Jesus on the shoulder. "You're a good guy, Jesus. One of the best I know. And don't worry, she sees it too. It was only a matter of time before you went home to see how your niece was doing. We all knew that before you did, I think."

"If you knew before this morning, then yeah, you did."

Adam laughed and pulled Jesus into a hug.

"Everything here will be fine. Go see your family and let me know if you need anything."

"I will, man. Thanks."

He washed his clothes, packed his bags, and called a ride-share. In the car on the way to the airport, it was late enough in the day that Stacey would be awake after closing the pub the night before, so he called. No answer. Then he texted. No answer. He tried to take his mind off her by calling a few regular clients that had appointments in the next few days to explain his situation. They were all very understanding, but when he got off the phone with them, there was still no response from Stacey, and he was at the airport.

His phone stayed silent through security and down the terminal. By the time he sat down at the gate, the silence was mocking him. He knew he was doing the right thing, but he wondered if Stacey would see it that way. If she continued to ignore him, would it be for one reason or the other? Or both?

Ugh. Women are hard.

The flight was uneventful, and when he landed, many notifications pinged his phone, but none were the one he was hoping for. At least the rental car was sweet. He'd miss his classic while he was in Texas, but there was something to be said for modern machines.

He drove straight to his parent's house and knocked. The door opened and a small, gray-haired woman rushed out and squeezed the life out of his intestines.

"Jesus! What do you think you are doing here?"

Her boisterous greeting made him smile. *"Hola, Mami.* It's good to see you too."

She ushered him in the house where his dad sat in his recliner.

"Well, this is a surprise, son."

"Hey, *Papi.* That was the idea."

"Sit. Sit." His mom pointed to the couch. "Do you want anything to drink? Are you hungry? You must've been traveling all day."

"Gracias, Ma, but I'm fine."

"Are you here about Mia? Her *tio* has always been her favorite."

"Of course. I'm everybody's favorite."

His parents just smiled at him.

"Luci called and basically told me to get my a... I mean, butt—sorry *Mami*—to Texas so we can all be together as a family. She also said something about me being the best, and it's not the same without me. Or something like that."

His dad chuckled and his mom rolled her eyes. It was good to be home.

After settling in at his parents' house, he drove over to his sister's place to surprise his niece. Ari opened the door and launched herself into his arms. It made him smile, just how alike his mom and sisters were.

"What are you doing here?"

"What do you think I'm doing here? I'm here to see how Mia's doing."

"You called to ask how she was doing yesterday."

"And now I'm here in the flesh."

Ari just smirked at him and ushered him inside. "Okay, a few ground rules. You'll wash your hands and sanitize them, and you'll wear a mask. And did you shower after you got off the plane?"

He quirked his eyebrow. "Yes."

"Good."

He followed Ari's directions before heading up the stairs to Mia's room.

"*Tio!*"

"Hey, Squirt! Tell me, does she make everyone sear the top layer of their skin off with scalding hot water before seeing you, or is it just me?"

Mia giggled. "No, it's everyone."

"Okay, good. It was worth it to see you, but now I don't have to be mad at her."

"Hey! You wanna play Uno? Mom never wants to play anymore."

"You probably beat her too many times. She never liked it when I beat her at games growing up either."

He winked and Mia giggled again. It was undeniably the best sound in the world.

She pulled the deck out and eyed him expectedly.

"Okay, Squirt. Deal me up."

It wasn't until she'd dealt out their first cards that he looked closer at them. "You have Harry Potter Uno cards? I didn't even know they made those."

"*Tia* Nat gave them to me when I started treatments."

"Well, they are awesome. I might have to get some for my place when I get back to San Diego."

She frowned. "When do you have to go back?"

"Not so soon that you need to worry about it. This will be a long visit, I promise."

She just nodded but didn't look convinced. He really did need to visit more often and stay longer when he did.

They played a few rounds. She won twice, and he won once, but he was pretty sure she let him win that last time because she felt sorry for him.

"Can I braid your hair, *tio*? I've been practicing for when mine grows back."

It was only then that he realized the beanie she was wearing wasn't hiding her hair. There was nothing left to hide.

"Sure, Squirt."

He pulled the rubber band out of his hair and sat with his back to her so she could reach the thick locks of his hair. While she worked on her braiding technique, he asked if she'd made any friends at the hospital, if the doctors and nurses were nice, and if she wanted anything special to help her pass the time when she was getting her treatments.

Her answers were vague and half-hearted, so he got the feeling she didn't want to talk about that stuff, and he changed the subject. He wanted to offer to take her to a treatment or two, but he needed to speak to Ari first.

"Did Mom tell you they're going to get me a wig?" She seemed excited at the prospect of wig shopping, so he didn't ask how she felt about getting a wig.

"No. That's cool. What color is it going to be? Let me guess. Purple!"

"No, *Tio*." She shook her head at him like he was so plebeian. "Brown. Like my hair was."

"Okay, you're right. That makes more sense."

"Plus, it's real hair that people donate. I don't think they even make purple wigs with real hair for kids. That'd be crazy."

"So crazy." He tried to do his best valley girl impression, and she giggled.

By then, she was done with his hair and yawning, so he took that as his cue.

"All right, Squirt. I need to go and spend some time with your *abuelita* before she accuses me of using her house like a hotel."

"Okay, *Tio*. Will you come by tomorrow?"

"Absolutely, as long as your mom says it's all right."

They hugged, and he went back downstairs where Ari was waiting for him on the couch.

Sitting beside her, he put his arm around her, and she leaned into him. Words weren't necessary as he held her. Neither they nor their family could predict the future, but they took hope in the fact that Mia seemed strong, and she was responding well to treatment.

"Mia said she's going to get a wig?"

"Yeah. Not that we get out much, but she gets stares when we do. If she didn't like drawing attention to herself before, she certainly doesn't like it now. At this point, I'll do anything to put a smile on her face."

Ari stifled a sob against his shoulder, and he hugged her tighter. She pulled back before he thought she should, but he knew better than to say anything.

"So, people donate their hair for these wigs?"

"Yeah, it's pretty great. Why?"

"Well, I got to thinking that maybe I could—I don't know—donate mine."

Ari gasped. "What? No."

"Are you saying I can't?" He chuckled at her reaction.

"Of course not. I just—your hair—it's beautiful. I can't even imagine you without long hair. I don't think you've cut it short since your Marine Corps days."

"All the more reason for a change. If I hate it, hair grows, but I want to show Mia that I support her. That I'm here for her every step of the way."

"Oh, Jesus. That's so thoughtful."

"Hey, where's Sam?" He just realized his brother-in-law wasn't around, and he'd never been comfortable with praise.

"It's Thursday. He's at work." She smirked at him like he was a doofus.

"Oh. Right. It's been a long couple of days. I thought it had to be the weekend by now. Who cuts his hair? Do you think they'd be able to fit me in this week?"

"Maybe. I'll call Ramon and see if he has any availability. Sometimes he'll squeeze a haircut client in the middle of another appointment. I'm sure he'll find time to help you donate."

"Thank you, sis. Could Mia come too? I didn't say anything to her in case it's not possible, but I think she'd like to be there."

Ari nodded. "I think you're right, but let's see if Ramon can fit you in first. I won't mention it to her until the day of the appointment, and even then, only if she's feeling okay."

"You're the boss."

"Damn straight."

They both chuckled at each other.

"Okay, well, I promised *mami* I'd be back for dinner. Can you let me know what Ramon says?"

"Absolutely, and thanks for coming over and seeing Mia. I'm sure she fell asleep once you came down, but she needs the visits."

"Well, I'll be back as often as possible while I'm here, and call me if you and Sam need anything. A date night. Someone to keep her company at the hospital. Whatever."

She walked him to the door and squeezed him hard in a hug. "Thank you, Jesus. I really appreciate you being here for us."

"Of course, *manita*."

Back at his parents' house, Stacey still wasn't picking up her phone and dinner wasn't ready, so he called Jeff to check in.

"Hey, Jesus. How's Mia?"

"I just got back from my sister's house. Mia's doing pretty good, all things considered, but I called to check on the studio."

"Man, don't worry about this place. We're good, and your clients will be here when you get back."

"I know."

"Or is it a certain manager you're worried about?"

He huffed. "Of course, I'm worried. She won't return my calls. She thinks I abandoned her. Now I've actually left the state."

"Well, don't worry about her either. She's digging her heels in. Already insisting on extra protocols and being a general pain in the ass." He chuckled.

"That's my girl."

"I'm inclined to believe she didn't do this, but that might mean we have a bigger problem on our hands."

"Yeah. I'm afraid it has to be one of the guys. Who else would know enough to convincingly frame Stacey like that?"

Jeff just grunted in response.

"I know that's why you wanted Stacey to be guilty. The guys have all been around longer. They're like family."

"I didn't want Stacey to be guilty. It just would've made this all easier. I'm used to replacing managers for one reason or another." He paused, and then chuckled. "Sounds dumb when I say it out loud."

Jesus laughed. "Well, it doesn't sound smart."

"Fucker." But Jeff was laughing too.

"Do me a favor and send me the login credentials for the cameras. I want to go over the video again. Maybe we missed something that will tell us who it really was."

"Sure thing. And no rush, but do you have any idea when you might be back?"

"Mia has two weeks left on her current cycle of chemo, so I'll stick around through the end to help my sister and brother-in-law out with the trips to the hospital."

"Okay, just let me know if that changes."

"Will do, man."

They said their goodbyes and hung up. With his attention no longer on the phone, he noticed many more voices coming from the family room than just his parents.

When he went to investigate, he was greeted by all four of his sisters, along with some of their spouses and most of their children. It was a full house.

"Jesus! *Hermanito*, you didn't tell me you were coming home!"

He hugged his sisters one by one while getting the third degree. "I didn't tell anyone, Nat."

"Wait. Why would he tell you and not me?"

"Because I'm his favorite, Mari."

Mari scoffed. "Whatever. Who cares? Why

would you want to be his favorite, anyway?"

He pulled Mari into his arms and squeezed her in a bearhug. "Aww Mari, don't be that way. My phone bill alone should tell you that I love you all equally."

She pushed him away as he chuckled, and everyone laughed.

"*Venid, mis criaturas, comed.*"

They found their usual seats around the large well-used, well-loved dining table when his mom called her "creatures" to come eat.

He looked around at his family and smiled. As a teenager, he'd considered family dinners an inconvenience when he'd rather been with his friends. However, as an adult, he realized how special that time was when they got together every Sunday and reconnected over a delicious meal.

"So, Jesus, tell us about this girl."

He looked at his dad in shock and then looked around at the rest of his family all smiling knowingly at him. What the fuck?

"Uh, what?"

"You don't think your sisters haven't all told us about the woman you're seeing?"

"I'm sorry, Jesus! They gave me *conchas!*"

He chuckled at Nat's outburst. He knew she couldn't resist the sweet cookies.

"It's all right, Nat. She's not a secret, but it might be a moot point, anyway. She's not returning my calls right now."

"What did you do?"

"What makes you think it was me, Ari?"

She gave him a look that their mother must've taught her.

"Ugh. Okay, fine. She discovered some missing money. When we checked the cameras, someone wearing her hoodie used her code to get into the building and accessed the safe in the middle of the night. We questioned her..."

"Wait. You questioned her? Like a criminal?"

"Not like a criminal, but yes, Mari, it's what we would've done with any other employee. I was trying to remain impartial."

"But you're not impartial. You're dating. No wonder she won't talk to you."

"Thank you, Nat. Very helpful."

"What happened after you accused her of stealing?"

"I didn't accuse her, Luci."

"Semantics. Then what?"

He huffed. "Then she wouldn't talk to me. I tried, but she blew me off. Now, she won't take my calls, and it's not like I can show up at her place while I'm here in Houston."

"Give her time."

"Thanks, Ari."

"I'm not done. Give her time, but when she's ready to talk to you, grovel. Grovel like you've never groveled before."

What did he say to that?

"I don't know this girl, Jesus, but real talk? You probably destroyed her trust in you. She was facing a scary situation. She needed you, and you weren't there for her. Not only that, but you were one of her accusers, even after she was the one who brought the problem to your attention. You failed her."

"Wow, Luci. Tell me how you really feel."

"I'm sorry, *hermanito*. I say this because I love you. If you want a real shot at patching things up with this girl, you must understand how far you've fallen."

He just sat there in silence as the rest of the family changed the subject and kept talking around him. Getting dressed down by his sisters at the dinner table was not what he'd expected when he sat down to eat.

More than ever, he needed to get a hold of Stacey to clear the air, or "grovel", as Luci put it. He just hoped she would eventually hear him out. What his sisters were saying wasn't anything Stacey hadn't already told him. They were just blunter about it.

Chapter Twenty-four

Stacey

Jeff didn't fire her, but he didn't make her feel secure in her place at the studio, either. She wanted to scream at the thief that put her in that situation, at Jesus for not having her back, and at the injustice of it all.

Every night, she was double, triple, quadruple checking her work, and whoever closed with her had to count the cash and sign the drop envelope with her. It was her idea, but Jeff told everyone that the change came from him. Since it came from the boss, no one outright refused, but some of the artists gave her shit for following his instructions to the letter. She wasn't about to lose the best job she ever had over something she would never do.

After two weeks, most of the artists were used to the new routine, and it gave her a chance to get to know them better. Beau was quiet, but sweet. He'd always been the most helpful with closing procedures and was the least disparaging about the change.

Dillion was the "class clown" type. He roasted her on the regular, and this was no different. Eric was still kissing ass to earn a permanent seat, so he was no trouble. He also had only closed with her one night when no one else wanted to stay until closing for walk-ins.

Troy varied wildly between joking with her about how dumb it was to whining that the process took too long. More often than not, he tried to talk her out of completing the steps at all.

The only one who remained openly hostile was Derrick. She got the feeling he was going through something–or maybe he was always an asshole–but closing with her was always a huge inconvenience to him.

She'd given away shifts at the pub to be able to close every night, and still only managed to close with each of them two or three times so far. It was hardly a large sample size to gauge reactions.

"When are you going to quit this, Stacey? I get it. You're not guilty, but I need help figuring out who is."

"And how do I do that, Jeff?" It was just the two of them at the front desk, and the whir of machines told her all the artists were tucked away at their stations and out of earshot.

"Tell me who doesn't like your new system."

"Well, they each had something to say about it the first time I made them double check the deposit. The only two who still don't like it are Derrick and Troy. Derrick grumbles about how long it takes. Troy tries to talk me out of it one way or another."

"That's hardly an admission of guilt."

Was it appropriate to say "duh" to your boss? Probably not.

"Okay. We're going to change it up a bit. Starting tomorrow night, don't ask them to check it anymore. You're not miscounting. You're not stealing. I know that. I trust you."

She took a deep breath. That was good to hear.

"I'll put a safe in my office before we open tomorrow. From then on, you're going to put the deposit in there. But you're going to leave a few hundred dollars in this safe." He pointed to the one under her desk. "Make it look like a real deposit, and we're going to see if anyone takes it."

"Okay. Can I ask why?"

"Turns out this wasn't the first time someone had come in after hours and stolen money. We just kept shit records at the time and didn't catch it."

She gasped. "What?"

"Yeah, Jesus had a hunch and has spent the last couple of weeks combing through a year's worth of video. Good thing the cloud backs everything up. To think I almost did away with some of those files to free up space. Anyway, he found a few other instances of a dark figure coming in to steal. I looked up the backdoor codes used at those times and they're all different. Someone must've figured out where I saved the list, so when this is all over, I'm moving that and giving everyone new ones, to say the least."

Completely dumbfounded by what she was hearing, she didn't know how to respond first to what she was hearing.

So, the problem started long before she came to the studio. She just found the problem that already existed. No wonder Jeff had finally decided to believe her. It wasn't anything she'd done.

The biggest news was that Jesus had been the one to clear her name. Maybe he hadn't totally abandoned her. Maybe she would've known that if she'd picked up any of his calls. He'd stopped leaving messages a week ago.

"Speaking of Jesus…"

Who was talking about Jesus? Certainly not her.

"I guess you already know this, but he's going to be back in a few days, so I need you to call the clients he canceled on and reschedule them. He said he would work open to close every day until he got caught up."

"Okay. Yeah, I can do that. Did he tell you exactly what day he was coming back?"

"No. He didn't tell you?"

"We haven't exactly…"

"You two still haven't patched things up?"

She just shook her head.

"I gotta tell you, Stacey. He's the only reason I didn't fire you outright. He insisted I hear you out. However, I also told him if he wanted me to hand this place over on a silver platter, then he couldn't play favorites with the employees. Even when he was dating one of them."

Her mind was spinning with all the new information, but mostly she just wanted to kick Jeff in the shins. A customer walking through the front door saved his legs.

"I'll call Jesus for a specific date while you see to this client and get back to you."

The next day, she'd just finished checking out a customer when Jesus walked through the front door. Or at least, someone who kinda looked like Jesus.

She was staring. She couldn't help it.

"Hey, Stacey. How are you?"

"I'm… good. Umm, how are you? Where's your hair?"

He threw his head back and laughed.

"What?" He touched his bald head, looking trepidatious. "Oh, this? You like?"

"Uh… yeah! Give me a second to get used to the new look." She paused and tilted her head back and forth as she looked him over. "It's different, but I love it."

He smiled wide as he walked closer. "For the record, you look good too, *mariposa*. I missed you."

She swallowed. She missed him too, but they had a lot to talk about. "How's Mia?"

"Doing well. She just finished a cycle of chemo and the doctors are optimistic. At this stage in the game, that's as good as the news can get."

"Oh, that's so wonderful to hear." She took a deep breath and asked what she wanted to ask.

"What are you doing tonight?"

"I only came by to make sure my station is ready for my first client tomorrow, so nothing important. What did you have in mind?"

"I'm closing tonight, but meet me at my place after?"

"I can do that, *mariposa*." He came closer, clutched her hand, and brought it to his lips.

As he kissed her fingers, her whole body grew warm. She'd never known what "swooning" was before she met Jesus. The stupid, charming bastard.

"Until later, *mariposa*."

He walked back to his station and left her alone at the front desk.

Later, she was at home when there was a knock on her door. She opened it to Jesus's smiling face. "Come in."

He walked in and made himself at home on her couch.

"Can I get you anything? Water? Beer?"

"No. I'm fine. Come sit with me. Please."

She sat, but they were both silent for a minute, neither knowing where to start.

"I'm sorry." They spoke at the same time.

They smiled at each other, but Jesus spoke next. "You have nothing to be sorry for, *mariposa*." She tried to interrupt, but he stopped her. "I should have handled that day differently. From beginning to end. You needed me, and I wasn't there for you."

"No. Let me stop you right there. I agree you

could've handled it better, but I could've too. I am not some wilting flower. Your support would've been nice. Telling Jeff where to stick it would've been nice. But it reminded me that I am perfectly capable of standing up for myself."

"You are capable, *mariposa,* but that doesn't mean you should have to face things alone. I am so proud of the strong woman you are. You may not need me to support you, but I hope you'll forgive me and allow me to be there for you when you could use someone to lean on."

She scooted closer to him on the couch, cupped his jaw and pressed a kiss to his lips. "I forgive you if you'll forgive me too."

He tried to speak, but she clamped a hand over his mouth. "Forgive me for not picking up when you called, for not returning your texts, and for giving you the silent treatment like a child when you were already dealing with so much."

"There's nothing to…" He stopped talking when he read the look on her face. "Of course, I forgive you."

She smiled and kissed him again before standing up and holding out her hand for him.

He stood but stopped her when she tugged him towards the bedroom. "I love you, *mariposa.*" She gasped. "I've been in love with you. My heart knew it, but it took my brain a minute to catch up."

"I…"

She paused, and he jumped in. "Please don't feel like you have to say it back. If you're not ready, that's okay. I'll wait as long as it takes."

"No. I... That's not..." She shook her head, hoping to get her thoughts in order. "I don't need time. I love you—I've loved you—too."

His entire face lit up in a smile before he kissed her. The kiss was slow and soft, and she sank into it like a cozy blanket in front of a warm fire. Neither of them in any hurry. The kiss wasn't a prelude to the main event. It *was* the main event. She wasn't just in love with Jesus—he was becoming like home to her.

They broke the kiss long enough to walk hand in hand to her bedroom, where they stripped down to their underwear and climbed into bed.

For hours, they kissed and talked before making love sometime before dawn and falling asleep. It was somehow more intimate than any night they'd ever spent together.

Chapter Twenty-five

Jesus

He sat up straighter on his stool and cracked his back. It'd been a week since he returned from Texas, and he'd crammed as many clients into that week as humanly possible. Maybe some even inhumanly possible.

"I think that about does it. You wanna take a look?"

"Hell, yeah."

He chuckled as he wiped down the completed bicep tattoo and backed up when the client stood to walk to the mirror hanging on the wall.

"Kick ass, Jesus. Just… awesome."

Lloyd was an eloquent one.

"I'm glad you like it. Come on, I'll get you wrapped up and out of here."

Lloyd paid Stacey at the front desk, and Jesus walked him out. Returning to the desk, he went around it and pulled Stacey into a quick kiss while they were alone.

"So, no one's taken the bait yet?"

She looked around his shoulder to confirm they were alone and out of earshot of anyone else. "No. Nothing yet. I'm not even closing every night anymore. Shouldn't they have made their move by now?"

"But Jeff and I are closing when you aren't. If anyone is as diligent as you are, it's us. Maybe we need to let the others have a turn before the person will try again."

"You're probably right."

"Ooo, say that again. I like it."

She swatted his arm. "Stop."

They were both laughing when the front door chimed, and Stacey turned to greet the client. "Welcome to Black Sails…"

The words dying on her lips brought his attention to the client who held a gun in Stacey's face.

"Give me the cash." The perp held out a sparkly purple gift bag.

Jesus took a split second to assess the perp. He was a nervous, twitchy mess, which was a terrible combination with a gun. He was also a kid, maybe fourteen or fifteen years old. Beyond that, though, he was clearly scared, desperate even.

He felt for the kid, but he loved Stacey, and her safety came first. He stepped in front of her while nudging her behind him. She huffed at him, and he would've smiled at that in any other situation.

"Okay." He took the outstretched bag from the kid. He would comply to end the situation easily.

A little money was not worth either of their lives. "Just lower the gun a little. You don't want to actually shoot anyone here today. Trust me."

"Fuck you. Just put the money in the bag!"

Jesus looked down at the register to pull out the bills. Just as he reached for the first stack of money, three things happened at once. Stacey shoved him hard, he heard a loud bang, and a scorching hot bullet whizzed past his ear. He hit the ground with Stacey landing on top of him, and the bullet lodged in the partial wall behind them.

Stunned, she didn't move for a second and he feared the worst until she looked up at him. He quickly checked her over for wounds.

"I'm not hit. I'm not hit."

He would be the judge of that, but he didn't say that out loud. After he checked over Stacey, he peeked over the front desk at the confused teenager who clearly hadn't meant for the gun to go off.

The noise brought all the other artists to the front. Jesus didn't think any of them thought it was caused by a gunshot until they got there and saw the gunman. They all retreated out of sight for cover except Troy, who stepped towards the dazed perp.

"Brad, what are you doing?"

"You're not supposed to be here!" The kid, "Brad" apparently, dropped the gun and fell to his knees, burying his head in his hands. "I'm sorry."

Troy placed his hand on Brad's shoulder, looked

back at Jesus, and sighed. "Do you plan to press charges?"

Jesus helped Stacey to her feet as he stood, then walked around the front desk and picked up the gun. It was a little out of curiosity, but mostly to secure the firearm in his possession, out of reach of anyone else. The gun was an older nine-millimeter and had clearly seen better days. "Depends on what you tell me right now. Where did you get the gun?"

Troy stood Brad up and put a protective arm around his shoulders, but Brad stared at the floor when Troy answered him. "That's the gun our mom keeps for safety."

"So, brothers then." He paused, and it all clicked. "*Esta pendeja*, you're our thief."

Troy hung his head like his brother. By then, the other artists had come out of hiding and someone behind him gasped.

"Wait, we have a thief?"

"Yes, Dillon. You didn't wonder why they started doing all these extra checks at closing?"

It impressed Jesus that Beau figured it out.

"I wondered. Just didn't think of that."

The guys chuckled, but Jesus wasn't in the mood to join in. This wasn't over.

"Why, Troy?"

"It doesn't matter now. If we promise to leave and never come back, will you not press charges?"

"No." He paused to let Troy and Brad sweat for a second. "No, I want to know what's happening. Then, I'll decide."

Troy took a deep breath and let it out slowly. "Our mom is sick and hasn't been able to work in a while. I moved back in to help with the bills, but it's still not enough. We're trying to move somewhere with a cheaper cost of living, but we haven't been able to save for moving costs. I didn't know what else to do."

"So, you stole."

Troy hung his head again. "Yes. I'm sorry."

"Why didn't you say anything to us?"

"Why would I? To whine? To cry on your shoulders?"

"No. If you'd just asked, we could've helped you. All the benefits we've participated in. All the charity food drives. You think we wouldn't help one of our own? Dammit, Troy! Stacey almost lost her job because of you, and I just want to punch you right now for all the shit you've caused."

It was a good thing Troy didn't open his mouth again or Jesus might've followed through on that punch. There wasn't anything he could say to make it better, but calling the cops wasn't going to do that, either.

He sighed. "Look. You're not forgiven–not by a long shot–but I won't call the cops. I won't be able to forgive myself either if I send you out of here, and you do some more stupid shit out of desperation. We'll get your family moved."

"What?" Derrick didn't sound thrilled.

Jesus turned to the other artists. "It's the right thing to do."

"So is calling the cops when someone shoots at you."

"It was an accident, and he's a minor. I will not ruin his future over this. Maybe you can handle that on your conscience, but I can't."

Derrick just threw his hands up in exasperation and walked away. Jesus turned back to Troy and Brad.

"Why are you doing this for us?"

"It's the right..."

"Thing to do. Yeah. I got that. But why?"

"Because I rebelled hard against my parents as a teenager and a young adult. If any of the many stupid things I did had gone on my record, I wouldn't have been able to join the Marine Corps. And the Marine Corps saved my life. Everyone deserves a little grace now and then."

Stacey's arms slipped around his waist, and she hugged him from behind. He took that to mean she supported his decision.

Chapter Twenty-six

Jesus

"**I**'m so nervous."

"Don't be, *mariposa*. My family already loves you more than me." He kissed her cheek as they walked up to his parents' front door.

She laughed. "I'm sure that's not true."

"Oh, it's definitely true!" His sister's voice rang from behind them.

"Thank you, Nat. Helpful as always."

"I know. Right? And you must be Stacey."

"Guilty."

Nat pulled her in a hug, and her breath whooshed out of her. "Nat, let up a bit. Don't break my girlfriend."

"No one's breaking, *hermanito*. Stacey, meet my husband, Leo."

Nat let Stacey go long enough for her to shake Leo's hand, and they all went inside the house together.

"Happy Thanksgiving, everyone!"

"Happy Thanksgiving, *mijo!*" His mom engulfed

him in a hug before turning to grab Stacey's hand and announcing her to the whole house. "And he brought his girlfriend! Everyone, meet Stacey."

"Hi, Stacey!" It was like they rehearsed it with everyone shouting at once, and she laughed.

"Why do I never get a welcome like that?"

"Come home more, *mijo*."

"Ouch, *Mami*."

Everyone laughed. He introduced Stacey around. She met Luci, her wife, Sarah, and their sons, Jason and Brayden. Then, Mari, her husband, Thomas, and their daughter, Elaina. He was introducing her around to some of his aunts and uncles who were there when a voice interrupted them.

"Look who made it!" His mom came up behind him holding an iPad. When he looked at the screen, Ari was staring back at him.

"*Hola, hermanito!* Happy Thanksgiving!"

"Hey, sis. Are y'all staying home today?"

"Yeah. We're having a small Thanksgiving here —just the three of us—but we'll FaceTime with you guys as much as possible."

"Okay, I wish you could be here, but I get it. Here!" He pulled Stacey into the shot with him. "Meet Stacey. Stacey, meet my oldest sister, Ari."

"Hello." Stacey waved at the screen and Ari brought her husband, Justin, and then Mia over to say hello.

"Mia, do you want anything special when I come over tomorrow?" He knew she'd be too exhausted for them to come over that day, but he wanted to see her.

"*Abuelita's* pumpkin pie." Mia leaned closer to the screen and whispered. "Mom's pie just isn't the same."

"Hey! I heard that!" Ari came up behind her. "But yes, I agree. Please bring the pie."

They laughed, said their goodbyes and ended the call, promising to call again after lunch.

It was probably the best Thanksgiving he'd had at home in years. For the first time, he felt like more of an equal with his sisters instead of just the younger brother. He'd always be the only boy, but he was no longer the only one still single. And if he got his way, he'd never be single again.

He touched Stacey's knee under the table. "Hey, sorry to spring that on you. Are you okay to go over to my sister's tomorrow?"

"Of course! I don't have any plans while we're here, and I'd love to meet them in person."

"So, you..." He didn't know how to ask. "You don't want to see any of your family while we're here?"

She smiled at him, but it didn't reach her eyes. "No. That's okay. They've made it very clear that they don't want to see me."

"I'm sorry, *mariposa*."

"Don't be. It's their loss. I made my peace with it years ago. Brenda is my family, and..." She put her hand over his resting on her knee. "You."

He leaned over and kissed her. It was chaste,

considering they were still at the dinner table surrounded by his family. "Yes, *mariposa*. You have me, and you have my family, for as long as you'll have us."

"Forever?"

He smiled ear to ear and kissed her again, holding her lips a little longer, the presence of his family be damned. "Forever and ever, *mariposa*."

Her smile matched his, and they probably looked like a couple of goobers with goofy, lovey looks on their faces, but he didn't care.

"I do have someone I want to see tomorrow if you don't mind making the time, but you don't have to come with me if you don't want to."

"Wherever you are, I want to be, too."

She kissed him again before they dug back into their meal. He'd be miserably full by the end of the day, but it would be totally worth it.

∞ ∞ ∞

Stacey

At Thanksgiving, she didn't tell Jesus who exactly she wanted to see, but that was because she didn't know how to.

Linda, her daughter's adoptive mom, reached out to her a few weeks ago, and invited her to come over the next time she was in Houston. They'd never made it a secret to Ally that she was adopted, but recently, she'd started asking more about her birth parents.

Stacey wondered if the day would ever come that Ally wanted to meet her, but she didn't expect it to come so soon. She expected to maybe meet Ally as a teenager, not an eight-year-old. Nervous didn't begin to describe how she felt, meeting Ally for the first time–kids were so honest–and she was also nervous to tell Jesus who she was meeting. What would he think? How would he react? Would he want to meet her too, wait in the car, or choose not to come with her at all?

He knew who Ally was. More than just the first time she told him the truth about her past, one night, she'd pulled out the box of photos she'd received over the years from Ross and Linda. They'd talked for hours about her daughter. He'd understood her continued conflicted feelings between missing her and knowing she made the right decision.

Standing at the patio railing with a cup of coffee in her hands, warm, powerful arms wrapped around her from behind. "What's on that beautiful mind of yours this morning, *mariposa*?"

She took a deep breath. Now or never. "Ally wants to meet me."

"What? Really? That's amazing. Wait. Is that who we're going to see today?"

"So, you still want to come with me?"

"Of course, *mariposa*. Wild horses couldn't keep me away."

So happy, she laughed as she turned around in his arms and buried her face in his chest. "I love you. So much."

"I love you too." He kissed the top of her head. "When are they expecting us?"

"Dinner Time."

"Okay, so we'll have lunch at my sister's and dinner with your daughter."

"Yay, more eating."

Jesus chuckled into her hair.

They got dressed and went to Ari's house. Sam, Ari and Mia were all wonderful. Just like the rest of Jesus's family, and she already loved them dearly like they were her own. Well, maybe better than her own.

When it was time to leave for Ross and Linda's house, her nerves kicked in. She grabbed Jesus's arm before he could back out of Ari's driveway. "I'm not ready."

He covered her hand with his and turned to give her his full attention. "*Mariposa*, you are the strongest woman I know. You can do anything you put your mind to. Do you want to meet her tonight?"

"I do. I really do, but what if she's disappointed? I won't be able to un-meet her if it doesn't go well."

"What could she possibly be disappointed about? You're amazing. You're funny, smart, beautiful, and you make a mean cocktail."

She laughed. "That'll come in handy in fifteen years."

"I can't promise tonight will go perfectly, but I can promise I'll be there every step of the way."

Her eyes threatened to swell up with tears, but she held them back because she didn't want to meet her daughter for the first time with red, swollen eyes.

"Let's go meet my daughter."

"That's the spirit, *mariposa*."

They pulled up to a beautiful home with a large, tree-covered front yard. It looked like something out of a fairy tale.

"Wow. They were living in a smaller house when I first met them. This is amazing."

"Looks like a great place to grow up."

"Yeah, it does. Doesn't it?"

At the front door, Jesus rang the bell as he grabbed her hand. She took a deep breath and waited.

The door swung open and instead of Ross or Linda, it was Ally. She was struck dumb and so surprised she forgot how to speak.

"Are you Stacey?"

"I... I am. Are you Ally?"

"I am!" Ally turned and yelled into the house. "Mom! Dad! Stacey and some man are here!"

Ross came around the corner. "Sorry! Ally is faster than me." He turned to his daughter. "Ally, you know you're not supposed to answer the door until you're tall enough to look out the peephole."

"I'm sorry, Daddy, but I knew it was Stacey!"

Ross ruffled his daughter's hair and turned to

Stacey. "It's good to see you again, Stacey." He turned to Jesus. "And who is this?"

"This is my boyfriend, Jesus. We just came from visiting with some of his family."

"Jesus? As in 'our Lord and Savior'?"

Jesus threw his head back and laughed. "Yes, just like him."

Ross chuckled too. "I'm sorry. I'm being rude. Please come in off the porch. Linda is just finishing up dinner."

He ushered them in, but Stacey couldn't keep her eyes off Ally. Pictures didn't do her justice. She was just so beautiful. Was it true or was there just something ingrained in parents to think their kids were the best? Either way, she didn't really care which it was.

"Stacey, I didn't know you were here already!"

She turned as Linda came out of the kitchen and pulled her into a hug.

"And who is this?"

"Linda, this is my boyfriend, Jesus."

"As in 'died on a cross'?"

She snorted. "Yes. He gets that a lot."

"I'm sure he does. Just 'boyfriend' and not more?"

She slanted a look at Jesus to see his reaction. Linda never had a filter, and it seemed like nothing had changed. "Well, I'm hoping he wants to be more."

He leaned over and kissed her. "He does."

Ross and Linda said, "Aww" at the same time,

and Stacey smiled back at them.

"Are you my birth dad?"

Shocked, she looked at Jesus–who looked just as shocked–before turning to Ally. "Oh, no, Ally. I'm sorry. He's not."

"So, who is?"

She looked at Ross and Linda before answering and they just nodded.

"His name is Robby. I haven't seen him in a few years, but I'll give your parents his information and maybe you can meet him too one day."

"Okay, Stacey. Thank you."

"You're most welcome, Ally."

When dinner was ready, they gathered around the dining room table and talked long past when their plates were empty. Ally was an amazing kid, and she'd never been so sure that she'd picked the right parents for her child than she was right then.

Epilogue

Jesus

Two Months Later

"It's perfect."

"It's haunted."

"Oh, hush. It's not haunted."

"Stacey, I have lived on this street for a long time, and it's been vacant for even longer than that."

"That doesn't mean it's haunted. Did anyone actually die there?"

"No. I don't know. Maybe."

"Are you afraid of little ol' Casper?"

"Not Casper, but maybe Bathsheba Sherman."

"Okay, valid." She laughed. "Come on, Jesus. It's in our price range, and it needs some work, but it's in pretty good condition, considering."

He was going to cave. He knew it. She knew it. It was only a matter of time. Plus, there wasn't anything else available on Melrose Lane at the moment, and there rarely was.

"Okay, *mariposa*. I'll think about it. Let's go back

to my place. Maybe you can convince me." He pulled her close and nuzzled her neck before they turned to walk back down the sidewalk.

A lot had changed in the last few months. Christmas had come and gone, but they'd flown to Houston to spend it with Jesus's family and seen Ally again. They'd even taken Stacey's aunt Brenda with them to meet everyone. She and his mom had hit it off immediately and traded phone numbers to keep in touch. He could only imagine what they talked about. Probably something along the lines of wedding colors and guest lists.

Jeff really had walked away from the studio and left it to Jesus to run. He still technically owned it, but he didn't care to be involved in the day-to-day operations. In fact, he and Stacey ran it together because he wouldn't have been able to keep his full schedule of clients while running the studio full time, and she was a natural at the business-side of things.

They'd successfully moved Troy's family to Arizona, much to Jeff's chagrin, but Jesus reminded him that it wasn't his problem anymore. Derrick was still an asshole, but he was a talented asshole who definitely wasn't stealing from them, so they put up with him.

The guys were much the same, though. Will and Nikki were settling into married life. Joe and his half-sister, Kaylee—Theresa and Blake's daughter—were growing like weeds. Adam still disappeared into his home office most nights and War still left for days on end for one protection gig or another.

Once back at the house that Jesus shared with his roommates, he didn't waste any time when he saw the house was empty. Throwing Stacey over his shoulder, he went straight to his bedroom and threw her on the bed.

She laughed. "Jesus! What are you doing?"

"Ravishing you. Isn't it obvious?"

"So obvious. You've swept me off my feet. Consider me ravished."

He chuckled as he removed her clothes and his. Before her, he would've never thought laughing during sex to be a good thing, but with her, everything was good.

Pushing her knees to her chin, he leaned down and sucked on her clit before running his tongue around and down through her folds and up again. Over and over before focusing on her clit as he used two fingers to enter her. He curled his fingers just enough to press up like he was reaching for the nub of her clit from the inside.

"Oh, Jesus. I love when you do that."

He knew that, but he had his mouth too busy to answer her.

"Oh, right there. Right there. Please keep going. Please. Please. Please."

He sped up his ministrations in response.

"Oh, fuck. I'm coming! Jesus! I'm coming!"

He kept going to draw out her orgasm, and when she was catching her breath, he blanketed her body and entered her in one thrust.

They moaned together as he moved, and she wrapped herself around him, plastering their sweaty bodies together. Stroking her clit, he wanted her to come again before he did. The feel of Stacey's sexy body brought him to the edge fast, and he was in danger of embarrassing himself. He was no two-pump-chump... unless Stacey was in his bed.

She cried out and his orgasm followed hers until they were both spent. Collapsing on the bed next to her, he pulled her into his arms, spooning her from behind.

"I love you, *mariposa*. I can't wait to spend the rest of my life with you."

He hadn't officially popped the question yet, but they'd talked about it enough that it was a foregone conclusion. He still wanted it to be special, though, and he would make it amazing for her. She deserved nothing less.

"I love you too, with all my heart, forever and ever."

Stay tuned for War's story, <u>Marine Protector</u>. The next full-length novel in the Melrose Lane series.

About the Author

Accountant by day. Writer by night. Mom always. According to my six-year-old's last Mother's Day card, I am in my forties, twelve feet tall, and "really good" at shopping. (Only one of which is true.) I'm in love with love, and in my stories, everyone finds their happily ever after. I'm living my own love story in a suburb of Houston, where some days I slay dragons and other days I read a whole book in one sitting.

Visit my website: https://authormkdwyer.com

Email me: author.mkdwyer@gmail.com

Join my **subscribers list**
https://authormkdwyer.com/subscribe

Social Media

Stalk me. hard

Friend me: www.facebook.com/mk.dwyer.737

Like me: www.facebook.com/author.mkdwyer/

Join my reader's group:
www.facebook.com/groups/
MelroseLaneBookClub/

Follow me:
Instagram: www.instagram.com/
Author.MKDwyer/
Twitter: www.twitter.com/AuthorMKDwyer
Pinterest: www.pinterest.com/AuthorMKDwyer/
Bookbub: www.bookbub.com/profile/MK-Dwyer
Goodreads: www.goodreads.com/author/
show/18363840.M_K_Dwyer
Amazon US: www.amazon.com/MK-Dwyer/e/
B07GX83BMQ
Amazon UK: www.amazon.co.uk/-/e/
B07GX83BMQ